This n...
HER ARDE...
by Kristi Gold,
meet Sheikh Ben Rassad—prince of Amythra,
man of mystery. This tall, dark, exotic oil mogul
was never in want of anything...until he rescued the
lovely Jamie Morris from harm and knew his life
would never be the same!

**SILHOUETTE DESIRE
IS PROUD TO PRESENT THE**

**Five wealthy Texas bachelors—all members of
the state's most exclusive club—set out to restore
the "Royal" jewels...and find true love.**

* * *

**And don't miss
TYCOON WARRIOR
by Sheri WhiteFeather,
the final installment of the**
Texas Cattleman's Club: Lone Star Jewels series,
available next month in Silhouette Desire!

Dear Reader,

Welcome to the world of Silhouette Desire, where you can indulge yourself every month with romances that can only be described as passionate, powerful and provocative!

Popular author Cait London offers you *Gabriel's Gift,* this April's MAN OF THE MONTH. We're sure you'll love this tale of lovers once separated who reunite eighteen years later and must overcome the past before they can begin their future together.

The riveting Desire miniseries TEXAS CATTLEMAN'S CLUB: LONE STAR JEWELS continues with *Her Ardent Sheikh* by Kristi Gold, in which a dashing sheikh must protect a free-spirited American woman from danger.

In *Wife with Amnesia* by Metsy Hingle, the estranged husband of an amnesiac woman seeks to win back her love…and to save her from a mysterious assailant. Watch for Metsy Hingle's debut MIRA title, *The Wager,* in August 2001. Barbara McCauley's hero "wins" a woman in a poker game in *Reese's Wild Wager,* another tantalizing addition to her SECRETS! miniseries. Enjoy a contemporary "beauty and the beast" story with Amy J. Fetzer's *Taming the Beast.* And Ryanne Corey brings you a runaway heiress who takes a walk on the wild side with the bodyguard who's fallen head over heels for her in *The Heiress & the Bodyguard.*

Be sure to treat yourself this month, and read all six of these exhilarating Desire novels!

Enjoy!

Joan Marlow Golan

Joan Marlow Golan
Senior Editor, Silhouette Desire

Please address questions and book requests to:
Silhouette Reader Service
U.S.: 3010 Walden Ave., P.O. Box 1325, Buffalo, NY 14269
Canadian: P.O. Box 609, Fort Erie, Ont. L2A 5X3

Her Ardent Sheikh
KRISTI GOLD

Published by Silhouette Books
America's Publisher of Contemporary Romance

Special thanks and acknowledgment are given
to Kristi Gold for her contribution
to the TEXAS CATTLEMAN'S CLUB: LONE STAR JEWELS series.

To the real "jewels" in this series:
Jennifer Greene, Sara Orwig, Cindy Gerard and Sheri WhiteFeather.
Thanks for taking me under your wings, and then letting me fly.
I couldn't have done it without you.

 SILHOUETTE BOOKS

ISBN 0-373-76358-1

HER ARDENT SHEIKH

Copyright © 2001 by Harlequin Books S.A.

This edition published by arrangement with Harlequin Books S.A.

® and TM are trademarks of Harlequin Books S.A., used under license.
Trademarks indicated with ® are registered in the United States Patent
and Trademark Office, the Canadian Trade Marks Office and in other
countries.

Visit Silhouette at www.eHarlequin.com

Printed in U.S.A.

KRISTI GOLD

began her romance-writing career at the tender age of twelve, when she and her sister spun romantic yarns involving a childhood friend and a popular talk-show host. Since that time, she's given up celebrity heroes for her favorite types of men, doctors and cowboys, as her husband is both. An avid sports fan, she attends football and baseball games in her spare time. She resides on a small ranch in central Texas with her three children and retired neurosurgeon husband, along with various live-stock ranging from Texas longhorn cattle to spoiled yet talented equines. At one time she competed in regional and national Appaloosa horse shows as a nonpro, but she gave up riding for writing and turned the "reins" over to her youngest daughter. She attributes much of her success to her sister, Kim, who encouraged her in her writing, even during the tough times. When she's not in her office writing her current book, she's dreaming about it. Readers may contact Kristi at P.O. Box 11292, Robinson, TX 76116.

"What's Happening in Royal?"

NEWS FLASH, April—Sources have linked the enigmatic Sheikh Ben Rassad, prince of Amythra, to Royal's own Jamie Morris. This mystery man is fairly new to Royal, and keeps to himself. The gossip mill claims he's filthy rich! And being the latest member inducted into the exclusive Texas Cattleman's Club gives him that extra cachet that's *so* irresistible to women....

Jamie Morris deserves some good fortune. Last we heard, she was jilted—before she even *got* to the altar—by her mail-order patron. Plus she was nearly a hit-and-run victim right here in town. Who could have wished her harm? Witnesses say the dashing sheikh came to the rescue...and has yet to release her from his protection....

And do our gentlemen in the Cattleman's Club wish to tell us about their secret meetings being held late into the night? More to come...

One

He had never seen anyone quite so beautiful, nor heard anything quite so intolerable.

Sheikh Ben Rassad pretended to peruse the antiques displayed behind the shop window as he watched the young woman walk away from the adjacent local dry cleaners.

She clutched a substantial garment covered in clear plastic—and sang in a pitch that could very well wake those who had long since returned to Allah. Ben would not be surprised if every hound residing in Royal, Texas—pedigreed or of questionable breeding—joined her in a canine chorus.

She sang with a vengeance, optimism apparent in her voice. She sang of the sun coming out tomorrow, although at the moment bright rays of light burnished her long blond hair blowing in the mild April breeze, turning it to gold. She sang as if tomorrow might not arrive unless she willed it so.

Ben smiled to himself. Her enthusiasm was almost contagious, had she been able to carry a decent tune.

As she strolled the downtown sidewalk, Ben followed a comfortable distance behind his charge while she searched various windows. Although she was small in stature, her faded jeans enhanced her curves, proving that she was, indeed, more woman than girl.

Ben had noticed many pleasing aspects about Jamie Morris in the weeks since he had been assigned to protect her covertly. His fellow Texas Cattleman's Club members had originally requested that he guard her against two persistent men from the small European country of Asterland. The men had been sent to investigate after a plane en route to Asterland had crash-landed just outside Royal—a plane Jamie Morris had been on. She'd been bound for her arranged wedding to Asterland cabinet member Albert Payune, a man with questionable intentions and connections. Jamie had walked away from the crash without serious injury or further obligation to marry. Although the suspected anarchists had returned to their country, she was still not safe. The marriage had come with a price. Quite possibly Jamie's life.

Because of Jamie's ties to Payune, Ben had secretly memorized her habits in order to keep her safe, guarding her with the same tenacity he utilized in business. Though she was a magnificent creature to behold, duty came first, something he had learned from his upbringing in a country that starkly contrasted with America and its customs.

Now he must protect Jamie from Robert Klimt, a man believed to be Payune's accomplice in planning a revolution in Asterland—a man Ben suspected to be a murderer and thief. Klimt had escaped not hours before from his hospital bed after languishing for weeks from injuries sustained in the crash. Obviously the club members had underestimated the man's dangerous determination, and Ben despised the fact they had not been better prepared.

At the moment, he needed to question Jamie Morris about the crash. Make her aware that he would be her shadow for however long it took to apprehend Klimt. Ensure her safety at all costs. In order to accomplish his goal, she would have to come home with him.

Carefully he planned his approach so as not to frighten her. Yet, considering all that she had been through the past few weeks, he doubted she was easily intimidated. And he suspected she would not like what he was about to propose.

But the members of the club depended on him. Little did Jamie Morris know, so did she.

Jamie took two more steps, stopping at the Royal Confection Shoppe not far from her original location. The song she sang with such passion died on her lips. For that Ben was grateful.

She stared for a long moment at the display of candies with a wistful look of longing. Ben studied her delicate profile, her upturned nose, her full lips, but he had never quite discerned the color of her eyes. He suspected they were crystalline, like precious stones, reminding him of his family's palace in Amythra, a place far removed from his thoughts more often than not in recent days. Reminding him of Royal's missing legendary red diamond and trusted friend Riley Monroe's murder. Reminding Ben of his mission: to find the missing red diamond and return it to its hiding place with two other precious stones. The jewels' existence had been known only in legend, but they were very real. The Texas Cattleman's Club members served as guardians over the heirlooms, as set out by the club's founder, Tex Langley. No member took the duty lightly, including Ben. And he was as determined to protect Jamie Morris in the process of recovering the jewel.

Jamie turned away, but not before Ben caught another glimpse of her plaintive expression. Then she began to whistle as she moved to the curb toward her aged blue sedan parked across the downtown street. He must make his move now.

The squeal of tires heightened Ben's awareness, the bitter taste of danger on his tongue. He glanced toward the grating noise to find that a car was headed in the direction of the sidewalk, aimed at an unsuspecting Jamie Morris.

His heart rate accelerated. Sheer instinct and military training thrust him forward, in slow motion it seemed. *Protect her!* screamed out from his brain.

As he reached Jamie, the vehicle's right front wheel swerved onto the sidewalk. Ben shoved her aside, out of danger, sending her backward onto the concrete in a heap. Her head hit the pavement with a sickening thud. The car sped away.

Ben knelt at her side, his belly knotted with fear—fear that he may have caused her more harm in his efforts to save her. "Miss Morris? Are you all right?"

When Jamie attempted to stand, Ben took her arm and helped her to her feet, relieved that she seemed to be without injury.

She grabbed up the bag from where it had landed next to a weathered light pole, brushing one small hand lovingly over the plastic. "I'm okay."

Concerned over her condition, he grasped her elbow to steady her when she swayed. "Perhaps we should have you examined by a doctor."

She stared at him with a slightly unfocused gaze and as he had suspected, her eyes were light in color, verdant, clear as an oasis pool. A smile tipped the corner of her full lips as she touched the kaffiyeh covering his head. "White

Sale in progress at Murphy's today?'' With that, her eyes drifted shut, and she collapsed into Ben's arms.

He lifted her up, noting how small she felt against him. Fragile. Helpless. Had he failed to protect her after all? If so, he would never forgive himself.

Lowering his ear to her mouth, he felt her warm breath fan his face. He laid his cheek against her left breast and felt the steady beat of her heart. A wave of welcome relief washed over him, and so did an intense need to shelter her.

A small crowd of Saturday-morning shoppers began to gather. Sounds of concern echoed in Ben's ears. ''Is that little Jamie Morris?'' someone inquired. ''Is she dead?'' another questioned. An older gentleman asked if he should dial 911.

''No,'' Ben stated firmly. ''I shall find her proper medical attention.''

Her injuries must be worse than they appeared, but at the moment he needed to get her away from the open street. Away from imminent danger. Although he had not seen the culprit, he knew who had been behind the wheel—Klimt— yet he did not know where he had gone.

Tightening his hold on Jamie, Ben crossed the street and headed for his car. She still clutched the bag, but her body lay limp against his chest.

Thankful that she was small, he laid her across the bench seat of his sedan and tossed the bag into the back. He quickly rounded the car and slid into the driver's side, grabbing for the cellular phone and hitting the speed dial to access Justin Webb's private number as he pulled away from the curb.

''Yeah,'' Webb answered, the noted physician sounding suspiciously as if he had recently crawled from bed. Ben suspected that either his new child or his new wife, had kept him up all night. He believed it to be the latter.

"We have a serious problem, *Sadíiq.* Someone has tried to run down Miss Morris in a car, then escaped."

"Is she okay?"

Ben studied Jamie's face resting near his thigh. Her eyes fluttered open, and she mumbled something he did not understand. "I pushed her away before he could do serious damage. She stood on her own before fainting, but she has struck her head on the pavement. At the moment, she is in and out of consciousness."

"Is she bleeding?"

Ben searched for signs of blood with one quick glance over Jamie's curled form. Blessedly, he saw none. "Not that I see."

"Can you rouse her?"

Ben shook her shoulder. "Miss Morris?"

She curled her knees farther into her body and her hands against her breasts. She smiled up at him for a moment before drifting off again.

"Yes. But she falls back to sleep. I will take her to the hospital."

"Don't," Justin said firmly. "If Klimt did this, then he could be waiting for you there. Take her to your place. Talk to her. Try to get her to stay awake. I'm on my way."

Ben clicked off the cell phone and tossed it onto the floor. He shook Jamie's frail shoulder again. "Miss Morris?"

"Hmmm…?" Her eyes fluttered open.

"Where are you injured?"

"I'm fine, just fine," she muttered, then inched closer to him and rested her head on his thigh, facing the dashboard, one hand cupping his knee beneath his djellaba.

She stroked delicate fingers up and down his silk trouser leg and mumbled, "Nice."

Ben's flesh quaked beneath her random touch. His thigh

muscles contracted, not in protest but in pleasure. He did not find her proximity nice at all. He found it intoxicating, as was the scent of roses filtering through his nostrils. And his thoughts at the moment were anything but nice.

"Mother."

Ben briefly took his gaze from the road and looked down on her innocent face and half-closed eyes. "What about your mother?"

She tried to raise her head then let it drop back into his lap. "Dress. Mother's dress."

Obviously she referred to the garment she had retrieved earlier. It must hold great sentimental value, the reason why she had made haste in reclaiming it from the sidewalk.

Ben laid a hand on her silky hair and stroked it gently. "Do not worry. It is here, safe from harm."

Looking somewhat satisfied, she turned her face and nuzzled her nose against him.

Precisely against the crease of his thigh, a place no female of good conscience would ever rest her face on a red-blooded Amythrarian male who had not been with a woman in a while. To Ben's misfortune, Jamie Morris was not thinking of his celibacy at the moment. She simply was not thinking at all.

He inched to his left. Jamie followed. He could go no farther without exiting the car. It seemed this predicament had forced him between a rock and a hard door.

Staring straight ahead, Ben commanded his desires to remain at bay. He attempted to concentrate on driving. Concentrate on getting her to safety. Concentrate on anything but Jamie Morris's face in his lap.

On the outskirts of town, where city dwellings and pristine lawns gave way to flat desert-like terrain, every curve of the rural road brought Jamie's face closer to dangerous territory—and Ben's tenuous control closer to snapping. He silently scolded himself several times. Scolded his weakness for this woman when he should be thinking of her well-being, not his stubborn male urges.

The white pipe-fence gates to the Flying Longhorn Ranch, his Texas home, could not have welcomed him any sooner. Fortunately, Justin Webb's sports car was parked in the drive, its owner standing on the porch leaning back against the Austin-stone facade, awaiting their arrival.

Gently moving Jamie's head aside, Ben slipped out and rounded the car to lift her into his arms. He strode quickly to where Webb was standing.

Once he was on the porch, Justin told him, "Take her inside."

Ben complied, carrying her into his guest room with Justin close on his heels. Inside the room, he carefully laid Jamie on the silk brocade spread covering the bed.

Justin pushed past Ben and perched on the edge of the mattress. Raising Jamie's blouse, he unsnapped her jeans and touched her abdomen in several places. "Her belly's still soft."

Ben imagined it was. Soft as the feather mattress beneath her. "Is that favorable?"

"Yeah. She's not flinching. No apparent tenderness."

Jamie tried to brush Webb's hands away and mumbled, "Leave me alone. I'm tired."

"I've got to do this, Jamie. Just hang on." Justin continued kneading her belly, examining her ribcage. He regarded Ben over one shoulder. "Help me get these jeans off. I want to check her limbs for possible broken bones."

Not normally reluctant to undress a woman, Ben found his own hesitation surprising, to say the least. "She stood after the accident. I believe that would indicate nothing is broken."

"That was adrenaline working," Justin said. "She might

have some swelling that could say otherwise. If so, we'll need to take her to the hospital.''

Ben felt as though invisible hands prevented him from moving forward. "I shall summon my housekeeper to assist you.''

Justin looked back with a frown. "Come on, Ben. I know you've seen half-naked women before. And I know you were guilty of getting them that way.''

Ben was without a response. His friend did not realize that, under different circumstances, undressing Jamie Morris would give him much pleasure. But he must resist the tempting thoughts. Now and in the future. If he desired to keep her safe, he could not allow the distraction.

While Justin slipped the denim down her narrow hips, Ben forced himself forward to remove her running shoes and tugged the jeans away from her slim legs. Immediately he averted his gaze from the thin scrap of white lace covering her womanly secrets. He cursed the carnal urges trying to surface. Cursed his sudden weakness where this woman was concerned.

Stepping away from the bed, Ben busied himself with folding the jeans in order not to stare at Jamie's lush body. After what she had unknowingly done to him in the car, the last thing he needed was to view Jamie Morris naked as a babe.

"No broken bones, as far as I can tell,'' Justin said. "She doesn't appear to be in any pain when I touch her. She does have an ugly bruise starting to surface above her hip.''

"My fault, I imagine,'' Ben said, keeping his eyes focused on a painting across the room as he laid the jeans on a nearby chair. "I pushed her harder than I'd intended.''

"You saved her life, Ben. Don't be so hard on yourself.''

Ben finally turned his attention back to the bed, grateful

the physician had covered Jamie's lower body with the spread.

Justin rummaged through the black bag he had brought with him and removed a stethoscope. He slipped it beneath the woman's blouse to listen to her heart. He then returned to the bag and drew out a small light, opening one of Jamie's eyelids, then the other, and shone the thin ray into each eye.

"Hey, are you in there, kiddo?" he asked.

Jamie opened her eyes, recognition dawning in their green depths. "Dr. Webb?"

"Yeah. The one and only. Can you tell me where you hurt?"

"My head hurts like a son of a gun," she muttered.

Justin raised her head up and examined her skull. "A nasty knot you got there."

"I'm just so sleepy." Jamie yawned and closed her eyes again.

Justin rose from the bed and faced Ben. "Her pupils are reactive, so she probably just has a slight concussion. You can let her sleep, but be sure to wake her periodically. Call me if she has any other symptoms, more pain, severe vomiting, or if you can't get her to wake up. I'm going to see what I can find out about Klimt."

Ben fought down the sudden panic. "You wish me to remain with her? Alone?"

Justin gave him a good-natured slap on the back. "Yeah. You can do it. I'm only a call away. If you even suspect her condition has worsened, then dial 911. The paramedics will be here in no time. But I'd bet she'll just sleep it off."

Ben respected his fellow Texas Cattleman's Club member and would prefer not to insult him. However, he still had questions. "Do you know this for certain? Forgive me, but you are a doctor who fixes imperfections."

"Believe me, Ben, before I took up plastic surgery and went into private practice, I saw my share of all kinds of trauma overseas. You have to learn to assess injuries on a moment's notice. Jamie will be fine. She's a tough kid. She's been through a lot lately. Probably exhausted on top of everything else."

Ben felt somewhat reassured. "Yes, I believe you are right. She stays up very late into the night, I have noticed."

Justin sent him a lecherous grin. "You've been taking this protection stuff pretty seriously, haven't you?"

Stiffening, Ben raised his chin, hoping to hide his guilt. "I was charged with protecting Miss Morris. I have been watching her, as you and the club members agreed I should." He would not admit that it had been his pleasure.

"Well, just keep doing what you're doing. I'll check back now and then throughout the evening."

As soon as Ben and Justin said their goodbyes, Ben quickly made his way into the kitchen to summon Alima. The housekeeper stood at the stove wearing stereo headphones, a habit she had recently adopted during most of her domestic activities. He doubted she even realized they had a guest.

Ben allowed her this concession, knowing it was futile to argue that she might miss the doorbell or phone if she could not hear due to the country-and-western music blaring through the portable CD player. At times he cursed buying her the gift for her sixtieth birthday. But he would do anything for her. She had been with him since his birth, and she was his only connection in America to his culture. He could not function without her care. Not unless he chose to have dinner at Claire's Bistro every day, or live in squalor.

Perhaps that was why he hadn't concerned himself with finding a wife. Alima provided for all his needs—except one. His thoughts turned to Jamie Morris and how she had reminded him that those needs had been neglected in recent months.

Wanting to get back to Jamie, Ben tapped his housekeeper's plump shoulder. "Alima."

She slipped the headphones away from her ears and released an impatient sigh. "Yes, Hasim. Lunch will be ready soon."

"That is not what I need at the moment. I need you to come to the guest room with me."

She favored him with a bright smile. "Is someone coming to visit?"

Alima enjoyed visitors, and lately there had been none, something she had mentioned often to Ben. He considered that as long as Jamie Morris was in his care, she could provide company for the older woman. "Someone is already here. Come." He gestured her forward and followed her to the room.

Alima's mouth dropped open once she saw the young woman lying in the bed in a tangle of sheets. The feminine attributes Ben had tried to avoid viewing were again exposed.

Ire turned Alima's eyes darker than moonless midnight. "Hasim! What have you been doing with this *bint*?"

"She is not a girl. She is a grown woman." Even to his own ears, Ben sounded defensive, as if he had engaged in disreputable acts with Jamie Morris. Admittedly, he had imagined a few in the car.

With a sigh, he turned his attention to Alima. "It is not what you think. She's been injured. Dr. Webb has examined her, and I am to make sure she is all right until she wakes. I believe she will be more comfortable if you undress her."

"It appears, Hasim, that you have already done that."

Ben clenched his jaw and spoke through his teeth, his patience now a slender thread on the verge of severing. "I did not undress her. Dr. Webb saw to that for the examination. Find something for her to wear, then put it on her." He pointed to the door. "*ruuHi!* Now."

Alima left the room, muttering a litany of Arabic curses followed by a prayer for Hasim bin Abbas kadir Jamal Rassad's wicked soul.

Jamie flailed about, twisting, turning, trying to escape the terrifying images.

The plane crash. The fire. Debris. Lady Helena's cries.

No. Not the plane.

A car coming at her. Flying through the air. Falling. Falling.

A stranger's arms around her.

She tried to sit up but couldn't. Someone held her down.

Fighting for her life, she balled her fist and struck out at the unknown assailant. An iron grip caught her wrist.

"Shhh, little one. You are safe now."

The voice wasn't threatening. More like soothing. A lover's voice.

Jamie blinked several times to focus and stared into a face that would make Adonis hang his head in shame. A white cloth of some sort, secured by a thin gold band circling his forehead, covered his hair but framed a strong jaw shadowed by whiskers. Mysterious eyes regarded her, the color somewhere between rich earth and molten steel. She saw concern and compassion there, and something familiar. But she'd never met him before. She'd definitely remember that, even though at the moment her memories were nothing more than fragments.

"Where am I?" she asked, her voice weak.

He loosened the grip on her wrist but didn't completely let her go. "You are safe."

Jamie tore her gaze away and did a frantic visual search of her surroundings. The room was a kaleidoscope of color and texture, from the rich aqua bedspread covering her to the ornate vases on the nearby black-lacquer end table. Tapestries hung from the bright yellow walls and pillows of every conceivable color rested on a white chair to her right. Sheer mosquito netting flowed beside her from the top of the bed. Practical, she thought, considering the size of the pests in Texas. Was she still in Texas?

No way. This was an exotic place. Beautiful. Foreign.

"Miss Morris, there is no need to be afraid."

He knew her name.

She stared at the stranger once again. Was this Payune? Had he had a change of heart and decided to marry her after all?

Not likely, and she certainly hoped not.

Payune was reportedly nearing fifty. This man was in his mid thirties at best. And his clothes would indicate that he wasn't from a small European country. They didn't wear robes and cover their heads in Asterland, did they? Of course not.

This dark, handsome stranger was Aladdin in his prime. Valentino reincarnate. A desert knight.

Oh, Lordy. She'd been sold into slavery.

A ridiculous concept, Jamie realized. But not as ridiculous as being sold like prime livestock into a marriage to a man she'd never met, arranged by her father for the sake of his failing farm. Had she been kidnapped by this stranger? Did he expect her to do his bidding, too?

Why not? He was practically lying on top of her, all hard, muscled male. Every inch of him, from his solid chest pressing into her breasts to his muscular thigh braced between her legs. Not to mention all points in between, some that were way too obvious not to notice.

Whoever he was, she intended to let him know up front that she didn't like being manhandled by strangers who had designs on her body.

Still pinned beneath his substantial frame, his face only inches from hers, Jamie struggled to squirm out from under him. The more she squirmed, the tighter his grasp on her wrists, the more aware she became of his strength...and his undeniable maleness.

"Be still, Miss Morris," he said, his warm breath drifting across her face, his low voice strained. "You will hurt yourself."

At the moment, she wanted to hurt him. Sort of.

Clenching her jaw tight, she spoke through her teeth. "I don't know what you're thinking, buddy, but if you expect me to be your love slave, then think again."

He looked altogether confused. "I am here to protect you. I need your promise you will not attempt to run away. Only then will I let you go and explain."

Whether or not she tried to run away would depend on his explanation. Still, she thought it best to agree. Considering how her luck had gone lately, she was prepared for anything. "Okay. You can get up now. I'll stay put like a good girl."

With a guarded expression, he unclasped her wrists and sat up but remained seated on the edge of the bed, leaving little distance between them. "I am Sheikh Hasim bin Abbas kadir Jamal Rassad, Prince of Amythra, currently residing in the city of Royal, in the state of Texas. You may call me Ben."

Thank heavens. No way could she remember all those names in her current state of mind. But now she remembered him. Or at least remembered hearing about him. The gossip mill claimed he was filthy rich. A mystery man relatively new to Royal, who kept to himself. A member of the exclusive Texas Cattleman's Club. But no one had bothered to mention his good looks. If you went for the tall, dark, exotic type.

"So tell me, Prince Ben, where am I?" she asked.

"You are in my house."

"And how, pray tell, did I get here?"

He rubbed his chin. "You do not remember the car?"

She searched her brain, an effort in pain thanks to her throbbing head. "I remember I'd just picked up the dress." *Her mother's dress.* She tried not to panic. "Where is the dress now? I have to know."

He laid a comforting hand on her shoulder. "It's hanging in the closet over there." He indicated two double doors across the room. "It is safe."

She felt somewhat better. At least the dress had survived. And so had she, for now. "I remember someone pushing me. Then falling."

"I'm afraid I was the one who pushed you to the ground. That is how you struck your head."

That explained her mother of all headaches. "Why?"

"To avoid the car coming at you." His face turned suddenly serious. "You are in grave danger, Miss Morris."

As if she couldn't figure that one out herself. "And what, exactly, does this have to do with you?"

"It was decided by the Cattleman's Club members that I should protect you. Your connection with Albert Payune has put you in a precarious position."

How much more bizarre could her life get? "Connection? We didn't have a connection! I've never even met the man."

"Once you are feeling better, I will explain further."

"I feel fine!" Jamie sat up in a rush only to encounter

a pounding pain in her skull and a wave of dizziness. She lowered her head back onto the pillow. "Okay, maybe not that fine."

Concern was reflected in his dark eyes. "Dr. Webb has examined you. He believes you suffer from a slight concussion. He ordered me to make sure you rest."

So she hadn't dreamed Dr. Webb's appearance after all. "He was here?"

"Yes. He checked you thoroughly and said you need to 'sleep it off.'"

Her eyes felt as heavy as two-by-fours. The same two-by-fours pounding her temples. "That's a good idea. Think I'll take another little nap."

The sheikh stood in one graceful move and hovered above Jamie, straight and strong and gorgeous beyond the legal limit. "I will be nearby. If you need anything, please do not hesitate to call for me."

Jamie felt a little woozy, but she didn't know if it was from the bump on her head, or the man standing above her. "Sure."

He studied her for another moment, sucking her in with those dark eyes, as if he were a human vacuum and she a tiny speck of dust. "I will make sure you are safe. As long as you are with me, no harm will come to you."

With that, he left the room.

Jamie stared at the door long after it closed, wondering how the heck she'd gotten into this predicament. Her father, of course. If he hadn't agreed to the blasted marriage arrangement, complete with a hefty reward, she would have lived the rest of her life never knowing anything about Albert Payune or Asterland. Or Sheikh Ben Rassad.

Okay, so maybe meeting the prince was a high point in all this mess. She had to admit he was definitely easy on the eye. A little too macho, maybe. But he had seemed genuinely concerned for her safety. Regardless, he still had lots of questions to answer, and soon.

Jamie yawned again. Too tired to think about anything but sleep at the moment, she closed her eyes and snuggled down into the soft bed, Prince Ben's words echoing in her ears.

As long as you are with me, no harm will come to you.

Amazingly, she did feel safe. Secure. Protected.

After sleep again overtook her, Jamie dreamed pleasant dreams, not nightmarish images of doom. She had visions of desert sand, starlit nights…and her role as the love slave of a sexy sheikh named Ben.

Two

The soft moans thrust Ben to his feet. He had dozed on and off while keeping vigil at Jamie's bedside but now found himself wide-awake, worried over her distressed state.

Lowering himself to the edge of the bed, he stroked her silky hair. "You are safe," he said softly. "I am here. No one will do you harm."

She continued to thrash and muttered, "Please."

A fierce surge of protectiveness streaked through Ben. Without thought, he slipped into the bed beside her and cradled her in his arms. She curled into him, her back to his front, fitting perfectly against his body. Although the room was dim, washed only in moonlight, he could see that the sheer muslin gown Alima had dressed her in rode high up her thighs. With one hand he drew it down, contacting smooth warm flesh. He quickly covered her with the satin sheet.

Torture, Ben thought. Or perhaps a test of his strength. Yet he was only a man, not superhuman, and his body reacted as any man's would. But he would not let her go until she had calmed. He'd simply think of other things aside from her petite body, her round breasts, her bottom only inches from treacherous territory.

He tried to recall his impending appointments. His investments. His upcoming summer trip to Amythra to visit his mother.

His mother.

She would most surely be shamed by his reaction to the helpless woman in his arms. She would expect him to be strong. Maintain a steel reserve. She was stronger than any woman he had known, except, perhaps, Jamie Morris.

Yet at the moment, Jamie seemed vulnerable. Quite different from the hellion who had tried to deliver a blow to his face earlier. The woman who had serenaded the population of downtown Royal without caring who might hear.

She was most definitely strong. Determined. And she would never fit into his culture for that reason. He had witnessed his European mother's struggles with his native customs on many occasions. But she had loved her husband dearly, and had adjusted as best she could. Now she was left alone in a place that still remained foreign to her, even after forty years. For that reason, Ben must visit her soon. After he was assured that Jamie Morris was safe.

Jamie stirred again, interrupting Ben's thoughts and driving him to the brink of insanity. Her firm buttocks wiggled against his very overheated manhood. As soon as she settled, he would leave her and return to the cold, empty chair, although that thought held no appeal.

Holding Jamie Morris did, and he cursed the fact that he had not been with a woman in quite some time. Surely this was the reason for his reaction. Weeks had passed since he had returned home. In his country, there were women readily available to care for his needs. Experienced women who considered taking him to their bed an honor because of his station. The couplings were without emotion and left him with a sated body and an emptiness deep in his soul. An emptiness he did not care to acknowledge.

Jamie Morris was different from those women. She aroused feelings in him that he had rarely experienced in his thirty-six years. Aroused his need to protect. To keep her safe. That desire lived so strong within him that he knew he would die before he let any harm come to her, if he could prevent it.

He had covertly watched her for several weeks, had memorized her habits. He knew she woke every morning at 6:00 a.m. and took her coffee and the newspaper onto her apartment's small verandah. She returned to the same spot every evening and stayed with a book late into the night. She was still very young, and he was very jaded. She was an innocent; he was world-weary. Yet at times he had glimpsed loneliness in her expression, as if she craved companionship. He could relate.

But he could not consider his loneliness tonight. He must remember his duty. He was here to protect her, not to sample her luscious body.

Ben sent up a silent prayer of gratitude when Jamie stopped moving, her breathing now deep and steady. At least she slept.

Ben, however, would not for quite some time.

The dream was so nice, Jamie didn't want it to end. The visions were so very real she could still feel her imaginary lover's arms wrapped around her.

Unwelcome light penetrated her closed lids and the fragrant smell of coffee teased her senses. Resisting the distractions, she snuggled further into the heavenly bed.

Her mind still caught in a pleasant haze, she reached for a blanket to cover her head. She contacted something that didn't feel the least bit like her grandmother's handmade quilt.

Her eyes snapped open. What the heck was that? She didn't own any pets. Her gaze traveled downward to discover exactly what she was clutching.

A hairy arm. A large hairy arm that certainly didn't belong to her—unless she'd grown a spare during the night. Definitely male, she decided, after surveying the golden skin laced with prominent veins, the large square fingers attached to the end of a hand. A nice hand. Very nice.

Nope, she knew where her arms were. Connected to her shoulders, not to her hip.

Coming fully awake, she sat up with a jolt and yanked the sheets to her chin. It was all coming back now, one frame at a time, like a slide show. She wasn't in her own bed, and she wasn't alone.

Who had relieved her of her senses? How could someone have crawled into her bed without her knowledge?

"What is going on?" she hissed, then cried "Ouch!" when she pushed farther back and her sore skull bumped the headboard behind her.

Only then did she realize that the arm was an extension of a real live half-naked man whom she didn't recognize, until she met his dark gray eyes now staring up at her through a fringe of sinfully long lashes. The man who had occupied her dreams.

Prince Ben, savior sheikh.

He slowly ran a hand through his thick mussed hair—hair as dark as the Texas crude that had made Royal so prosperous. "Did you sleep well?"

Now suffering from sexy sheikh shock, Jamie couldn't force herself to utter one word.

When she continued to stare at him, his mouth curled up in a smile that revealed deep grooves framing his mouth and enhanced fine lines around his eyes. A smile that would melt an iron washtub. Dark whiskers scattered above his well-defined lips and granite jaw made him look a bit on the sinister side. Sensually sinister. She figured he probably had to shave twice a day. A beard like that would definitely promote whisker burn during long kisses. She'd just bet he could kiss the bloomers off Betty Mays, Royal's spinster county clerk.

And he was in bed with *her*. Jamie Morris, who didn't even kiss on the first date.

"Well?" he asked, his voice deep and raspy.

"Well what?"

"Did you sleep well?"

"Yes, thank you." She had found her voice, but where was her brain? This was no time for pleasantries. "No! I mean…why are you in bed with me?"

He rolled onto his back and stacked his hands behind his head, giving her an intimate view of the tuft of hair under his arm. Jamie looked away and contacted his bare chest. Her gaze followed the path of dark hair that began as a silken mat between his pecs then thinned to a stream over his abdomen before disappearing into the waistband of a pair of striped pajamas. And just below that…

Oh, my.

Like someone viewing a horror film, Jamie didn't exactly want to look, but she couldn't tear her eyes away from the hypnotic sight, even if her life depended on it.

Suddenly realizing he was speaking, she pulled her gaze back to his face. His grin deepened, causing her cheeks to fire up like Manny's grill at the Royal Diner.

"You were having bad dreams. I worried you might hurt yourself if you thrashed about too much."

She didn't remember a single bad dream. A very good dream, yes. "Oh."

"So I took the liberty of holding you until you calmed. I apologize if my presence in your bed has alarmed you."

"I wasn't alarmed exactly. Just a bit unnerved." Jamie was still unnerved, but she wasn't suffering from fear, as he'd assumed. She was more afraid that her dreams had been real, and he wasn't telling the absolute truth.

She chewed her lip for a moment, trying to decide how to broach the subject. Asking point-blank seemed like the sensible solution. "Did we..." How could she ask him *that?*

He impaled her with his night-sky eyes. "Did we what?"

Do the wild thing. Make whoopee. Shuffle the sheets.

She couldn't force herself to say any of those things.

He had the nerve to smile again. "I am waiting."

Jamie got the distinct feeling he enjoyed watching her squirm like a night crawler on the end of a hook. "You know...you and me...together. In the bed."

His smile disappeared, replaced by a dark, sensual expression even more disarming. "Did we make love?"

"Yeah. Did we do that?"

"Why would you assume this?"

She didn't mind mentioning the dream, but she refused to reveal that he was the prime subject. "Well, because I was out of my head. And you are in bed with me. And then I had these images of hands...and things." Lots of things.

"Someone hurting you?"

"No. Just the opposite."

He rolled to his side and faced her again with his elbow bent, one palm bracing his cheek, his eyes darkened by something Jamie couldn't quite name. "Do you mean hands touching you? Perhaps a mouth on you, kissing every inch of your body until you writhed with pleasure? Someone making love to you until you could not breathe, yet you wanted more, until you found yourself begging for the very thing you feared, giving everything over to sensation until you were lost, body and soul?"

He spoke in a low steady tone that made Jamie shiver and sweat, all at the same time.

She somehow managed to speak, with effort. "Yes, something like that."

His smile crept in once again, slowly, and only halfway. "No, Miss Morris. That did not happen between us. If it had, you would know. And you would not so easily forget."

Without further comment, he pushed himself up and left the bed with graceful movements, like a panther progressively stalking its prey. And Jamie sat with her mouth gaping like a sprung screen door, feeling as boneless as putty, her body immersed in heat and her head reeling from his words.

As he walked to the chair across the room, Jamie couldn't help but notice the way his pajamas tightened with each stride, revealing a bottom that would best be described as a true work of art. He picked up a heavy blue robe and slipped it on, covering his artful bottom, much to Jamie's disappointment.

He faced her again, this time his expression all-business, unreadable. "You must be hungry. I will have my housekeeper bring you a tray so that you may regain your strength."

She would need all the strength she could get to fight his control over her. Her desire to know him. All of him.

Shaking off the covers and the stupid thoughts, Jamie

scooted to the end of the bed and touched her toes to the luxuriously carpeted floor. She needed to get out of here. Away from him. The danger she might face outside was nothing compared to the danger this man posed to her sanity and her sudden urges. "Yes, I'm starved. But I can eat after you take me back to my apartment."

"I am afraid that is not possible."

"Why not?"

"You must remain with me until we find the man who is attempting to do you harm."

Jamie stiffened her frame and tried to stand. She felt weak as a newborn, every inch of her crying out in protest. One giant total body ache. Bracing her hand on the bedpost, she steadied herself to keep from falling in front of the man. She refused to let him believe that she couldn't take care of herself.

"Look, Prince Ben, I'll be fine. If anything happens, I'll call the police." Her spongy knees didn't want to support her.

He stepped toward the bed and caught her elbow when she leaned a bit. "You cannot do that. We cannot involve the police at this time."

This guy had too many rules, none of which she understood. He also radiated a sensuality that wasn't easy to ignore.

She stared up at him, only then realizing he was tall. Very tall. Intimidating-to-the-max tall. "Care to explain why I can't call the cops?"

"Trust me, Miss Morris, this is for your sake. The less you know, the better that will be."

Jamie decided he was sorely mistaken, and his determination to keep her in the dark grated on her already raw nerves.

Oh, well. She'd play along for now. She was too tired

to argue. "Since I can't go home just yet, mind if I use your facilities?"

His dark brows drew down with confusion. "Facilities?"

"Bathroom? I'd like to freshen up."

"Of course. I thought you might want to bathe, so I had my housekeeper set out some things for you. This way."

He held on to her arm as he guided her to the room across the hall. Once they reached the door, she expected him to leave. He didn't.

With her hand on the knob, she gave him her best sugar-sweet smile. "Am I allowed to have some privacy?"

"I thought you might wish me to draw your bath."

"So you can watch?" Jamie cringed. She sounded like she wanted him to watch.

He smiled and Jamie felt it down to her size-five feet. "However tempting that might be, I will allow you your privacy after I help you prepare."

"I'll manage. I'm feeling much stronger." *Liar, liar, pants on fire.*

"As you wish. If you find you do need help, there is an intercom near the tub—"

"I can handle this. I promise."

She backed into the room and slammed the door in his face. Slammed the door on those mysterious eyes and all that out-there sexuality. Turning, she leaned back against the wooden surface for support. But it wasn't the lump on her head making her feel like an overcooked noodle. *He* made her weak knees weaker and her shaky body shakier.

Determined to drive him out of her mind, Jamie concentrated on the huge room. A room big enough to house Sadie, her trusty blue sedan. An opulent bath straight out of her fantasies of what a bath should be.

Several black marble steps led to a mammoth whirlpool tub, a huge arched window its backdrop. The matching

marble vanity top was graced with gold fixtures and two
basins complimented by jeweled soap dispensers and toothbrush holders. And laid out near one sink—for her benefit,
she presumed—was a brand new toothbrush and toothpaste
and two velvety black towels with a matching washcloth.
On a freestanding gold rack near the toilet hung a lush red
velvet robe and underwear. Her underwear.

Her underwear?

She reached back and planted both hands on her butt.
No lines. No underwear. She wore nothing more than a too-
large sheer ecru gown. The armholes, big enough to drive
a truck through, hung all the way down to her waist. No
wonder she was shivering.

Who had relieved her of her white lace drawers? And
why had she just now noticed?

She'd been barely coherent, that's why. And obviously,
the cad had undressed her. Bared her bod and taken liber-
ties.

No way. He hadn't done anything lewd to her person.
No doubt about it. Like he'd said, she would know.

Recalling his suggestive words, the thought of him undressing her again caused shock to course through her already shocked body. And it annoyingly excited her.

Regardless, she planned to have a serious talk with the
sheikh. Planned to inform him that, at the very least, undressing her without her permission was ungentlemanly.
She valued her privacy, and although she wasn't all that
modest, she did have high standards and certain expectations. If someone was going to get her naked for the first
time, then she darn sure better be conscious during the process.

A wave of nausea hit her like a raging bull. She slumped
onto the step and considered the intercom.

No. She could do this.

With stilted motions, she managed to draw a bath and slip into the tub without passing out. The warm water soothed her sore limbs and made her feel a bit more human.

After luxuriating for a while, then attending to all her toiletries, Jamie felt halfway decent again. Now all she needed was some food, and to convince the sheikh that she needed to go home. But how could she do that in just a robe and underwear? Where had he hidden her jeans and shirt? Okay, so maybe he hadn't hidden them, but she wouldn't be a bit surprised if he had. No clothes, no escape. Obviously he was determined to keep her here against her will.

Well, Prince Ben was wrong if he really believed he could do that.

She slipped on her underwear and the robe, then opened the door and tried to gauge where she should begin in order to find him. Starting down the hall, she peered into several rooms, all bedrooms decorated in more bright colors, but she didn't come upon the man with many names, and probably many talents.

At the end of the corridor, wonderful smells drew her forward. The kitchen must be close, and maybe she would find him there. But before she reached her destination, she came to a den. It gave new meaning to the term *great room*.

The place was a combination of luxury and comfort. Old West meets Middle East. A set of horns hung near the vaulted ceiling over the massive white-rock fireplace, and, draped below, a purple tapestry with rainbow colors woven throughout traveled down the stone wall to the top of the hearth.

Jamie moved farther into the room and noted another opening and a hallway that seemed to go on for miles. In the immediate area, several chairs and rugs were set out in various locations across the gleaming hardwood floors, all in elegant dark colors. The whole place was velvet and marble, a sprawling ranch house most would only dream of, and something she'd not been exposed to in her twenty-two years. She had always appreciated simple. She liked simple. Not that she couldn't get used to luxurious.

Scanning the area, she honed in on a huge suede caramel-colored sofa set to one side of the fireplace. And in the middle of that sofa sat a man, reclining against thick cushions, reading a newspaper, his long legs stretched out before him, booted heels propped on the heavy oak coffee table. He wore jeans and a T-shirt. Threadbare jeans. Tight T-shirt.

Considering his lazy posture, his common ranch-hand clothes, he could be just any sexy-as-sin cowboy. But when he looked up, nailing Jamie with those iron-gray eyes, there was no mistaking his identity.

Prince Ben as Bad-Boy Cowboy.

Ben stared up at Jamie now looming over him dressed in an oversized robe, her eyes flashing anger, her delicate jaw set tight. He suspected she would soon demand more answers from him. Answers he was not at liberty to give her.

Tossing the paper aside, he dropped his feet from the table and straightened. "You are looking much better. Refreshed." With her damp hair falling just below her slender shoulders, her face freshly scrubbed, she was all softness and innocence. A celestial being.

"How dare you!"

She no longer looked angelic. She looked as angry as Alima when a tennis championship interrupted her American soap operas.

What had he done now? "I do not understand."

She clenched her fists and Ben braced for another swing,

but fortunately it did not come. "How dare you undress me and put me in that see-through gown. I have never in my life—"

"Miss Morris—"

"—met a man who thought—"

"Miss Morris—"

"—he could get away with taking off my clothes without me knowing it and—" She put a hand to head and looked as though she might faint.

He vaulted off the couch and circled his arms around her to prevent her from falling. "Miss Morris, you must calm down. You are still not well."

She looked up at him but did not push him away, or try to punch him. Instead, she leaned into him. "I'm fine, thank you very much!"

She did not seem fine. Her skin was pale, almost translucent, and she looked as though she might buckle. "I think not." He tightened his hold on her.

"I want to go home," she said willfully, belying her fragile state.

"I told you that is not possible."

She locked into his gaze, her chin raised up in determination. "You can't keep me here."

"I am hoping you will see that it is necessary in order to ensure your safety."

"I'll tell you what's necessary. I need to find a job." She grasped the front of his shirt. "I'm running out of money. My rent's due right now. Then the car payment." She sounded desperate, her voice pleading.

He rubbed her back to comfort her, all too aware of her breasts pressed against him. The way she smelled, fresh and clean. Womanly. He held her closer to anchor himself. "I will provide for you until the time you can return to your apartment. I will arrange to pay your debts and see to it that you are comfortable in my home for now.''

She stiffened in his arms. "I don't need your charity. I can take care of myself."

Her attitude was the very reason he had never been involved with an American woman. Although he admired her independence, he did not always understand it, just as he did not understand his mother at times. Pride would not keep her safe, but he could. He would. "We will consider it a gift."

"A loan," she corrected, seeming to give in.

A strong sense of satisfaction settled over Ben at the prospect she would agree to stay with him, at least for now. "We shall discuss your financial situation later."

She relaxed somewhat. "Can I at least go home and get some clothes?"

"I will find you appropriate clothing."

"I have to feed...uh...my fish."

He took her arm and led her to the sofa, then brought her down next to him. It seemed best to put some distance between them. Simply holding her again resurrected more unwanted feelings within Ben. Feelings he did not welcome but could not seem to stop. Yet he must halt them. Remember his duty to her.

He sighed. "I will take you to your apartment where you can feed your pets and gather some clothes. But you must agree to come back with me."

Her smile traveled all the way to her jewel-like eyes, causing Ben's pulse to race out of control. "Okay. Then it's a deal?"

"Yes, but first you must eat."

She shrugged. "I'm not sure I'm all that hungry."

He was, but not necessarily for food. He stood before he

lost his head, his control. "You can eat something. I shall summon Alima."

She slumped back onto the sofa. "Alima?"

"My housekeeper." And oftentimes thorn in his side.

Jamie shrugged again. "Okay. Does she do hot dogs? I'm really craving a hot dog."

Ben smiled in response. "I will see what I can do."

He then departed for the nearby kitchen to seek out Alima, glancing toward the sofa in the event Miss Morris should change her mind and try to escape. He hated holding her captive, and had he been less honorable, he might have led her to believe he *was* her captor, and she his slave. But honor was something his parents had instilled in him from birth, therefore he had no choice but to tell her the truth. As much of the truth as he could allow.

Alima was opening the oven door, removing fresh-baked bread. She turned around and tossed the pan onto the stove, then slipped the headphones away from her ears. "Is our guest awake now?"

"Yes. And she needs nourishment."

She lifted the lid from a heavy black pot on the stove. "I have prepared *simich* in a very hearty stew."

The wonderful bouquet made Ben's mouth water. "She does not want fish stew. She has requested a hot dog."

Alima narrowed her dark eyes. "I do not prepare hot dogs."

"You will prepare something like it. She is our guest."

She slapped the lid back on the boiling pot. "I will prepare something American, but I do no hot dogs."

There was no sense in arguing with her. With Alima, he chose his battles carefully. He would need her assistance with Jamie in the future. No matter how stubborn Alima could be at times, she was a kind woman. She had a way with people, able to soothe them during dire moments. Jamie would need Alima's kindness, for if she caused more trouble, put herself in more danger, then he would not be able to be kind.

"Bring the food into the living room on a tray," he said. "We will dine there."

"Do you wish the stew, Prince Hasim, or do you prefer the Texas food?" Her tone implied once again that she didn't approve of his burgeoning American tastes even though she was guilty of the same.

"I will have what Miss Morris is having."

Alima strolled to the refrigerator, muttering in Arabic under her breath as she yanked open the door and peered inside.

Ben returned to the living room to find Jamie curled up on the sofa, her eyes closed. But when he approached her, she quickly came awake and sat up. "I'm sorry. I just can't shake this sleepiness."

He still worried over her condition even though he had spoken with Justin several times by phone since the day before. The doctor had assured him that Jamie would be weak for a few days, but not to worry. Ben did worry, although perhaps he should be thankful she wasn't quite recovered. The potential for her to fight him would increase with her strength.

He joined her on the sofa. "Alima will bring you something satisfactory. I am afraid we have no hot dogs."

Jamie yawned. "That's okay. Right now I think I could eat just about anything if it stood still long enough."

"Then your appetite is returning. This is good."

She smiled. A pretty smile that withered Ben's insides like blades of grass in the sweltering Texas heat. "Yep. I'm feeling better," she said. "And right after lunch, you can take me to my place."

He should expect her persistence in this matter. She was not one to give up easily. "All right."

She smiled. "You promise?"

At the moment, he would promise her anything. "You have my word."

With her head lowered, Alima scurried into the room carrying a tray full of meats, cheeses and breads. She slipped it onto the table before them but did not raise her eyes to Jamie until Ben said, "Alima, this is Miss Morris."

Jamie held out her small hand to Alima. "You can call me Jamie."

Alima did not take the hand Jamie offered, as that would be disrespectful, but she did afford Jamie a smile. "I am pleased to have you in Prince Hasim's home, Miss Morris. If you wish anything, please let me know." She turned to address Ben. "Would Miss Morris be more comfortable dining at the table instead of here in the *mayaalis,* with the dead animals?" She gestured toward the cowhide rug draped on the floor in front of the hearth.

Ben repressed a chuckle. Jamie did not.

"I believe Miss Morris and I are quite comfortable here." He regarded Jamie. "I am afraid Alima has never approved of informality. She believes that my mother spoiled me by letting me run the palace, doing as I pleased."

Alima departed, muttering in her native tongue all the way to the kitchen.

"What did she just say?" Jamie asked.

"The monkey is a gazelle in the eyes of his mother. An Arabic proverb."

Jamie laughed, a rich vibrant sound that made Ben want to laugh with her. "I have to remember that. Maybe while we're stuck here together, you can teach me some Arabic."

There were many things he would like to teach her, the

least of which involved his native tongue. Or perhaps it *would* involve his tongue. And his hands, his body...

Thrusting the thoughts away, he said, "Arabic is best learned in an atmosphere where it is readily spoken. I only speak it with Alima on occasion and when I return home."

She took some meat from the tray and shredded it, then nibbled a few bits. "Where is home?"

"Amythra. A small country near Oman."

She took another bite and spoke around it. "Well, I'm not good at geography, so I'll take your word for it."

Ben placed some of the fare on his plate and opted to use a fork, unlike Jamie who used her fingers, licking them on occasion, causing a rising heat to stir low in Ben's belly.

He ate in silence while watching Jamie put her all into the meal. She ate as if ravenous. As if it were her last bite.

He suspected she approached most everything with heart and soul and unyielding determination. He imagined she would approach lovemaking the same way.

Again his body stirred, and he cursed the fact he had not dressed in his djellaba. American jeans could not hide his sins should he lose control over baser urges.

Crossing one leg over the other, he pushed his plate aside and leaned back against the sofa. Jamie did the same.

"That was wonderful," she said, rubbing her belly.

Ben visually followed the movement of her hand, imagining his own hand there.

He looked away, questioning his wisdom. How could he not touch her if she lived under his roof? How could he continue to ignore his desires if she was with him every waking moment?

He must. He would call on all his strength and avoid situations that might threaten his control. At one time he had not been in control, and his own father had paid the price. He had vowed then that never would he let anyone harm a defenseless human being, especially one he cared about. And he was beginning to see Jamie in that category, no matter how inadvisable that might be.

Needing to get away, he rose from the sofa. "Are you finished, Miss Morris?"

She stood. "Yes. And if you'll point me in the direction of my clothes, I'll change and we can head to my apartment."

"You will find your clothes in the top drawer of the bureau in your room. Alima has laundered them for you."

Again she smiled. "How nice. Remind me to thank her."

"Yes, and I will change, too."

When she stood, the robe gaped open, revealing the valley between her breasts. "Change into what?" she asked.

Into a madman if she did not close the robe. "My traditional dress." He reached for the robe and she stepped back. "I am trying to cover you."

She looked down. "Oh. This thing is too big."

He suddenly realized that not only would she be more comfortable in her own clothes, *he* would be more comfortable if she was wearing them. At least somewhat.

She crossed her arms over her breasts, much to Ben's relief—and disappointment. "Don't get me wrong, Ben, but wouldn't you be a little less obvious if you stayed in what you're wearing now? I mean, you're trying to protect me. When in Rome and all that jazz."

He bristled at the jab, although he believed she meant nothing by it. "It is expected of me," he explained. "Both in the business world and in my country. I have promised my mother that I will keep this connection to my birthright."

She looked away. "I'm sorry. I didn't mean to offend you."

"No offense taken. There are many things about my culture that most Americans do not comprehend."

She locked into his gaze and he saw true sincerity in the green depths of her eyes. "I'd like to understand."

In that moment, he had no doubt she would.

All their differences seemed to melt away, and Ben wondered if she would be the kind of woman who would understand him. Understand his ways. Understand the man beneath the prince.

Impossible dreams.

Three

Jamie relished the feel of the warm April sun filtering through the car's tinted window, the lush leather seat beneath her. The black sedan was the ultimate in luxury. Masculine, sleek, like its owner.

She regarded Ben with a sideways glance. "I like your wheels. But wouldn't a truck be more practical on a ranch?"

"I own two trucks. I travel in this because it's safer."

"Safer?"

"Bulletproof."

Bulletproof? Did he have a price on his head, too?

Jamie took in a deep breath and pulled a leg underneath her. She turned toward him as much as the seat belt allowed. "Why on earth do you need a bulletproof car?"

"Because of my family's influence, there are people who exist for the sole purpose of doing us harm. But since I've been in America, I have encountered no trouble. I have sent most of my bodyguards back to Amythra for that reason.''

Bodyguards and bulletproof cars. Obviously Prince Ben was important. A somebody. Royal, Texas, was full of somebodys. As a fourth-generation Royal native, Jamie's father had once been a respected farmer. But Caleb Morris had squandered that respect with frequent gambling and drinking binges since his wife's death. Jamie missed her mother, too, but her father still hadn't come to terms with his loss.

He was probably in Vegas now, blowing the money he'd earned for selling his daughter into marriage instead of taking that money and trying to salvage the farm. At least Payune had been gracious enough to let them keep the marriage funds for her ''inconvenience and mental anguish,'' after he'd decided to void the contract.

She didn't consider an emergency plane landing a mere inconvenience or simple mental anguish. It had been terrifying. Although she was grateful that the wedding had never happened, she didn't have a dime to show for all her trouble. Her daddy had taken every last cent.

Burying the anger as she had for the past few months, Jamie glanced at Ben again, his eyes hidden by dark sunglasses. His features were angular, his nose sharp but not overly big. And oh, that kiss-me-quick mouth.

A classically handsome man. A man many women would want, not only for his good looks, but also for his wealth. She wondered why a good-looking prince with lots of money had never married. Then it occurred to her. Maybe he *was* married. To some woman back in his country. Maybe to several women. Did they still do that? Someday she'd find out more from Alima. But if the housekeeper was anything like her employer, Jamie realized that might never happen. So she might as well jump at the chance to find out for herself while the opportunity existed.

"Are you married, Ben?"

"No."

"Have you ever been married?"

"No."

A man of few words when it came to his personal life, she decided. "You don't have a woman waiting for you back home in your country?"

"No, I have no one waiting for me there."

"A girlfriend here?"

This time he smiled. "No, not here, either."

For some reason, that fact relieved Jamie. And her relief annoyed her. She wasn't about to play the role of his girlfriend while he insisted on handing out demands and trying to control her life. Like he'd really want her, plain old Jamie Morris from the country. "Don't you need some kind of heir? I mean, don't people who have royal blood need that?"

"My older brother, Kalib, has taken over the rule of Amythra since my father's death. He has five sons. Enough to supply Amythra with all the heirs my country will ever need."

"So while you were at home and your brother was having kids, what did you do?"

He fiddled with the radio and tuned it in to a station playing light jazz. "Before I came here to complete my education, I served as a commander in my country's military."

"Oh. So that's why you're so into this protection thing."

"I have been taught to protect those who cannot help themselves. Helpless women and children."

That made Jamie sit up straight and grit her teeth. "So you think all women are helpless?"

"Not all," he said, looking straight ahead.

"Good, because we aren't all frail little creatures waiting to be rescued."

"I would not assume that about you, Miss Morris. I believe there are times when you can take care of yourself." He glanced at her for a brief moment. "And times you cannot."

"And you can?"

"Yes. Many things are done out of necessity. Defending what you believe in to the death. Resorting to whatever means necessary to protect those in your care."

He said the words with such conviction, Jamie was determined to find out more about this overwhelming need he had to save everyone. "What do you mean by 'whatever means necessary?' Hurt someone? Maybe even kill someone?"

He shot another look in her direction then brought his eyes back to the road. "Yes. If necessary."

The admission hung over the car like a shroud. The images bouncing around Jamie's head were anything but pleasant. She deplored violence of any kind. But she found it hard to believe, considering his kindness to her that Ben could hurt anyone. "Have you had to do that? Hurt someone?"

His hands tightened on the steering wheel as if he had them around an imaginary neck. "Whatever I have or have not done in the past does not matter now. What matters is that I keep you safe."

The hard set of Ben's jaw told Jamie not to press, but she wondered if, in fact, he *had* hurt someone. Maybe even killed someone. Someday she'd ask again, but not now. Considering the way he continued to white-knuckle the steering wheel, obviously she'd already said too much.

Riding in silence, they passed through town on the way

to Jamie's apartment. A few tourists, mostly antique enthusiasts, occupied the afternoon streets. Retired folks who'd blazed the unbeaten path that took them to the small community of Royal, a place rich in oil, folklore and legend, and rich in rich people. Home to up-and-coming businessmen and women. Jamie's hometown that had changed and grown to suit the times. But she hadn't changed all that much. Not as much as she'd wanted. And now the prospect of returning to college to get her nursing degree seemed as far away as Ben's homeland.

When they passed the cleaners, Jamie suddenly remembered Sadie. "Where's my car?" She stared out the window and saw only an empty space where she had last parked. "Oh, heavens, they probably towed it. I can't afford to get my car out of the city lot—"

"Your car is safe."

Jamie leveled her gaze on Ben. "How do you know?"

"I have it stored in a garage at my ranch. One of my workers retrieved it at my request."

The man had considered everything. Taken care of everything. "Thanks." It was all she could think to say.

Once they pulled into the drive at the Royal Court Complex, Jamie quickly slid out of the car. But before she could make her way up the stairs, Ben grabbed her arm and stopped her progress.

"Wait," he said. "I must go first. Stay behind me."

Jamie opened her mouth to protest, but snapped it shut. She might as well let him have his way. His mother-hen attitude was something she'd have to learn to live with for the time being. She didn't have to like it, though.

Jamie let him pass and followed him up the stairs and into the hall, surprised that he went straight to 3C, her apartment. He withdrew her keys from his trouser pocket and held them up for her to indicate the correct one. She probably should be surprised he knew where she lived, that he even had her keys, but she wasn't. Nothing he did from this point on would shock her. In fact, she figured after everything that had happened—the stupid marriage agreement, the plane crash, the almost-hit-and-run, nothing would ever shock her again.

She was wrong. So wrong. When Ben pushed open the apartment door and she saw her upturned couch, her shattered floor lamp, her kitchen drawers tossed aside like yesterday's garbage, shock wasn't even close to what she felt.

"Don't move," Ben hissed, causing her knees to lock in place like the Tin Man without his oilcan.

He put up a hand, a silent command for her to wait on the threshold while he investigated. Blinding fear caused her temples to throb and her body to tremble. Not fear for herself. Fear for Ben. What if someone waited for him? What if several intruders ambushed him?

Jamie tried to convince herself that he would be fine. He had military training. But as far as she knew, he was unarmed.

A shaky breath of relief seeped out when Ben returned to the living room, all in one piece, and gestured her inside. "He is gone."

Moving forward on rubber legs, she took in the sight of her ransacked apartment. Nothing had been left in its place. Not one magazine, not one knickknack. Almost everything had been either destroyed or tossed aside, including much of Jamie's heart when she noticed her grandmother's porcelain angels in pieces scattered about their curio-cabinet home. Keepsakes passed on to Jamie's mother, then Jamie, and intended eventually to be passed down to Jamie's child. A symbolic death of a dream. Jamie's dream.

"Oh...no...not...." She bent to survey the horrible debris. How could anyone be so heartless? Why would anyone want to do this to her? What had she done to them to deserve such cruelty?

She fought back angry tears. Fought back sadness and frustration and a total feeling of helplessness.

"Jamie."

At first she didn't realize it was Ben standing over her, Ben calling her name. Then gentle fingertips circled her arms and lifted her up. Up into his strong embrace, his protective arms. He soothed her with words, some spoken in his native tongue, a language she didn't understand, but they made her feel safe.

Jamie clung to him, letting the tears come, unheeded, unwanted. She pressed her face into the fine silk of his robes, allowing his comfort. But only for a moment.

Pushing out of his arms, she let anger take the place of tears. "Damn whoever did this. Damn him to hell and back!"

Ben's dark serious expression stopped her ranting cold. "Did anyone give you anything when you were on the plane?"

Her mind was a muddled mess. As trashed as her apartment. So why was he asking about the plane? "What do you mean?"

"Were you given anything? An envelope? A package? Anything at all?"

"No."

"What about your luggage?"

"Destroyed in the fire. Every last shred of it."

He dropped his arms from around her and paced the room. "Did you have a bag with you that you carried off?"

"No. I had nothing with me but my mother's wedding dress."

Ben's gaze snapped back to her. "Did you have it with you at all times?"

"Yes. I was holding it when the plane made the emergency landing."

He walked back to her. "Was it out of your possession at any time?"

Why was he so interested in all these things? "I don't understand why you're asking me this."

Ben shook his head and paced some more, as if his thoughts only came if he kept moving. "There is something missing. Something we believe the man who did this is looking for. He thinks you have it."

Jamie stomped her foot, frustration replacing her grief over the break-in. "What is this something? Maybe if I knew, then I'd know if I have it."

"I cannot tell you. And if you had it, you would know."

Jamie rolled her eyes to the ceiling. "Oh, wow. I didn't know you spoke in riddles, too." She hugged her arms to herself, hating all the secrecy. Her father was a master at secrecy.

Ben stopped his pacing and faced her again. "I am sorry I cannot tell you more."

"Sorry?" She clamped her mouth shut against the oath threatening to spill out. "This is crazy. I'm just a good ol' Texas girl who made the stupid mistake of letting her father manipulate her into a marriage. All of a sudden, I'm thrust into some crazy scheme about some missing *something* and now I've got a target on my back."

"I will make certain he does not harm you."

The whole concept was so ludicrous, Jamie wanted to laugh. "You and who else?"

He seemed unaffected by her near hysteria, or her sarcasm. "If you would like to retrieve some clothes to take with you, I will escort you to your bedroom, then we must leave here. You may also bring your fish if you would like."

She would like to add foolish to frustrated since she'd been both. Not to mention frightened. Might as well tell Prince Ben the truth, even if he wasn't willing to do the same. "I don't have any fish. I made that up so you'd bring me back here. Seemed like a good idea at the time."

Ben smiled. A knock-your-feet-out-from-under-you grin. "Well, Miss Morris, you are very creative."

Darn him! Jamie couldn't help but smile back, although what she really wanted was to sit down on the floor, throw a tantrum and have a good cry. If there was such a thing as a good cry. Instead, she chose to look on the bright side. If Ben hadn't come to her rescue the other day, then this could have happened while she was in the apartment, alone. She might have been hurt again, or worse. And now he was offering to keep her safe and give her a place to live until... Until what? Would she ever really be safe again?

She couldn't worry about that now. She'd consider that later. Right now she wanted to grab some clothes and get out of here before the robber came back to finish the job, meaning finish her.

"Okay, let's go find some clothes." She stopped at her bedroom door, but didn't turn around. "And I really like it better when you call me Jamie."

"All right then...Jamie."

Pleasant chills coursed up Jamie's spine when he said her name. She sensed his closeness, felt his heat even though he remained a step behind her. And she wondered if being with Sheikh Ben Rassad was such a terrible thing after all.

In the back conference room of the well-appointed Texas Cattleman's Club, Ben affected attentiveness while listening to his fellow members discuss the recent events. In reality, impatience rushed through him as his thoughts turned to Jamie. He needed to get back to her immediately. Although he had put his workers on alert and posted a guard at the door, he would not feel at ease until he was with her again, seeing to her safety himself.

"Is that right, Ben?"

Ben's gaze snapped to Justin Webb when he realized the doctor was addressing him. "I am sorry. What were you asking?"

"The color of the car. Was it white?"

With a sigh, Ben leaned back in the chair. They had been through this before. "Yes. It was white."

"Winona did some checking for me," Justin said, referring to his wife who was also a police officer. "According to her, a white car was stolen from the hospital lot, the day Jamie was almost run down, so it's a safe bet Klimt was driving. They found the car abandoned right outside town, but we're pretty sure he wasn't strong enough to get too far on foot because of his injuries. He's still around here, somewhere."

Ben straightened again, thankful Justin's wife continued to keep them informed. "Yes, there has been no doubt in my mind from the beginning that Klimt drove the car and that he is still a threat to Miss Morris."

Aaron Black sat forward. Ben noted the diplomat's concerned expression and knew more questions about Jamie were forthcoming. "Have you asked her about the diamond?"

"Not specifically, since I believe the fewer who know about the diamond, the better. I have asked if she was given anything before boarding the plane. She says no."

Dakota Lewis frowned. "And she is absolutely sure, beyond a doubt?"

Normally the comment would not have bothered Ben. Lewis was retired from the United States Air Force, trained in the art of interrogation. Yet the need to defend Jamie burst forth and Ben could no longer control it. "Of course, I believe her. She has been through much. I do not care to upset her further by asking again and again."

Justin raised both hands, palms forward. "Whoa, Ben. We're not saying you should harass the woman. We just want to be sure she's not forgotten anything."

"She has not forgotten."

Matt Walker, Ben's neighbor and closest friend in America, finally spoke. "Okay. The diamond's still missing, and for some reason Klimt thinks Jamie has it. We just don't know why."

"And it's good he thinks she has it, even if she doesn't," Dakota added. "If he's connected to the revolution as we now suspect, selling the diamond is his only chance to raise money since we've recovered the emerald and opal. He'll eventually try to get to Jamie again and that's the way we'll catch him."

Ben narrowed his eyes. "Like a helpless lamb waiting for the slaughter?"

"We'll make sure that doesn't happen, Ben," Justin said. "But we have to find the diamond, and with any luck, return it to its rightful place, here with the others." He pointed toward the plaque in the grand salon that covered the hole in the wall containing two of Royal's legendary jewels. The third was still missing.

Peace, Justice, Leadership; the club's mantra etched across the plaque reminded Ben why he must endure the questions. Why he must see this through, not only for Jamie's sake but also for the town's prosperity.

"We need to put Klimt away for good," Matt said, "and we can't do that unless we find the man. I agree that he'll try to get to Jamie again. Unless he found what he was looking for in the apartment.'' He rubbed his jaw. ''Maybe he hid it there.''

''I don't think so,'' Aaron said. ''He's been hospitalized since the crash. When would he have had the opportunity?''

''The night he killed Riley,'' Justin interjected.

''*If* he killed Riley,'' Dakota said. ''We don't know for sure it was him.''

''It was him,'' Ben said adamantly. ''But I do not think he would have hidden the jewel in Jamie's apartment since she was home the night before the wedding. The luggage would have been a more likely hiding place. After all, the other jewels were found on the plane. I believe that the diamond was somewhere in her luggage and was perhaps lost in the fire.''

''We've looked in what was left of her luggage,'' Aaron added. ''We didn't find it. And we went over every inch of that plane.''

Justin leaned back in his chair and clasped his hands behind his head. ''Looks like we have no choice but to wait it out. See if he comes after Jamie again. If he doesn't, then he's found it and could be on his way back to Asterland. If not, he's still looking and that means Jamie's still in danger. If so, he'll try to find her, you mark my words.''

The thought of Klimt harming one golden hair on Jamie's head made Ben stifle an oath. He shoved back his chair and stood. ''If he touches her, I will kill him.''

The vow echoed in the room, all its occupants' eyes now trained on Ben.

Ben moved away from the table. ''I must return to her now. I will stay in touch.'' With a quick bow of his head, he took his leave, but not before he heard Matt's familiar Texas drawl.

''Yep, he's got it bad for her, all right. Let's just hope

his feelings don't interfere with him keeping her safe, and helping us get that diamond back.''

The words followed Ben all the way through the ornate grand salon and out the door. The overcast skies suited his black mood. He welcomed the impending thunderstorm that would truly complement his emotional turbulence.

The members were wrong. He would not allow Jamie Morris to keep him from his duty. He would prove to them he could resist all temptation, and that he did not have it ''bad'' for his charge. He was simply honor-bound to protect her. That was all it was or would ever be.

And that was what he told himself over and over, all the way home.

One minute he was vowing to protect her, the next minute he was gone.

Jamie walked aimlessly around the living room, not knowing what do about her situation. She'd tried to read some magazines to entertain herself, wishing she could turn back time. Wishing it was still December and she still had her old job back. Wishing she was living in her simple apartment and her only worry was trying to keep her dad from sinking farther into debt and depression. Wishing it was before the blasted notice had been posted all over town announcing Bride Wanted for Albert Payune of Asterland.

Never had she felt so alone, so out of place. Where was Ben now? Off planning her future? Deciding her fate?

He'd left an hour ago, barking demands about her staying inside. Staying away from the windows and doors.

Well, there wasn't any reason why she couldn't just take a peek outside. See what was going on. Surely there would be no harm in that.

Quietly she approached the front window and pulled back the heavy beige curtains. A man sat on the front porch, kicked back in the wooden glider with a shotgun resting across his meaty thighs. A Santa belly hung to his lap, probably the result of too much chicken-fried steak and beer. His ratty straw cowboy hat dipped low on his forehead, covering his eyes. Eyes that were closed, Jamie suspected. The piece of hay drooping from his mouth suddenly did a nosedive when his lower lip went slack.

If this man was Ben's idea of protection, Jamie would be better off with her own gun. Maybe she couldn't shoot straight to save her hide, but at least she wasn't napping.

Dropping the curtain, she stretched and braced her hands on the small of her back. She wasn't as tired as she had been, but she still felt the effects of getting up close and personal with the downtown sidewalk. The bruise on her hip was just plain ugly now, but the knot on her head had all but disappeared.

She felt bored, restless, in dire need of some kind of physical activity. She doubted Ben owned a treadmill, although he must do something to keep in such superior physical shape. Probably just came naturally for him, though. She couldn't imagine him dressed in gym shorts, working out at the local Y. Now another kind of workout she definitely could imagine.

My, my, Jamie Morris, you are turning into a bad girl.

The little voice in her head sounded remarkably like her grandmother. But her Nana had been gone for some time now, as had Jamie's own mother. Still, she thought about them often. Many times she had craved the company of a woman. Craved some honest-to-goodness motherly advice. Like now.

She suddenly considered Alima.

Would Alima talk to her? All she could do was try. It beat the heck out of talking to herself.

Jamie strolled toward the kitchen. Considering the spicy

smells coming from that direction, she figured she'd find the housekeeper there. She stepped into the room to find Alima busy at the island counter, chopping vegetables with a vengeance, her ears covered by bright yellow headphones.

Walking to the counter, Jamie stood in front of Alima in hopes of getting the woman's attention without scaring the wits out of her. After several minutes had passed, she tapped her on the arm.

Alima's gaze darted up from her task, and she stripped her ears of the headphones. She lowered her eyes. "I am sorry, Miss. I did not know you were standing there."

From the sound of the music coming through the headphones dangling about the housekeeper's neck, Jamie could understand why. She smiled at the woman. "Is there anything I can do to help you?"

Alima looked almost alarmed. "Oh, no, Miss. It is my duty to serve you. You must rest."

Jamie frowned. "I'm not even tired. Actually, I'm tired of resting. I'm about to go nuts just sitting around doing nothing. Surely you can think of something."

Alima surveyed the kitchen then pulled a barstool back from the island. "You may keep me company."

Conversation wasn't exactly a physical activity, but Jamie supposed it would have to do. Besides, she could find out more about the sheikh. She took her perch on the barstool and considered how she could do that. She guessed just coming out and asking would be the best place to start. "So, Alima, how long have you known the prince?"

Alima sent Jamie a kind smile. A mother's smile. "Since he was an infant. I cared for him then, as I care for him now."

"What about his mother?"

Alima's knife stopped in mid chop. "Her Highness cared

for him as well, but she had many duties to attend to and was in need of my assistance.''

"And you followed him here?"

"Not in the beginning. When he was still at the university I remained in Amythra. When he bought this house,'' she made a sweeping gesture around the room, her voice full of disdain as if it were below princely standards, ''he sent for me to attend to him here in America.''

"Where did he go to school?"

"The University of Texas in the city of Austin.''

Jamie smiled. From now on, she would think of Ben as Lawrence of Longhorn instead of Arabia. "That's interesting. Do you have children of your own?"

A sadness passed over the woman's expression. "No, Miss. Prince Hasim is the closest I have to a child. Allah did not see fit for me to bear children, but he was gracious in allowing me to care for the sheikh.''

A lump formed in Jamie's throat when she thought about her own mother, how much she had cared for her, coddled her and loved her. Jamie had been so very, very lucky. And seeing Alima's face, the maternal pride when she spoke of Ben, made her realize how much she would value having a child. Later. Much, much later.

The sound of a slamming door caused Alima to look up from her chopping and Jamie to slide off the barstool, ready to go for the nearby butcher knife in case the unknown apartment destroyer might come strolling in.

Instead, Ben entered, his face all hard lines and angles. His expression relaxed somewhat when his gaze contacted Jamie's. "I see that you are safe, no thanks to J.D., my slumbering guard.''

Jamie laughed. She couldn't help it. "Yeah, I noticed J.D. was snoozing.''

Ben's face hardened once again. "Did you go outside after I told you not to? Do you have a death wish?"

"I went to the window—"

"Did I not tell you to stay away from the windows?"

"I just took a peek—"

"That peek could have cost you your life!"

"But it didn't."

Ben turned away in a swirl of white and black robes as he left the room. Furious, Jamie followed. Of all the stubborn, hardheaded sheikhs she'd ever known...

Lord, she didn't know any other sheikhs except this one. But she had known stubborn men, namely her father. And the best way to deal with them was to let them know point-blank that they didn't have the upper hand.

"I'm going crazy!" she shouted at Ben's back.

He spun around to face her, fire in his steely eyes. "Better crazy than dead."

Jamie braced both hands on her hips, expecting steam to pour out of her ears at any moment. "Well, I might as well be six feet under the way you've made me a prisoner here."

In a rush, Ben grasped her arms. "Do not say that. Do not ever say that!"

Jamie tried to move away, but his grip tightened. "You're hurting me."

He finally dropped his hands. "I am sorry, but this is for your own good. This man will stop at nothing to get to you." At least he looked somewhat contrite.

"Who is this man?" she asked, hoping now he would give her just a clue.

"The man who wishes to hurt you."

Jamie rolled her eyes. "So we're back to that again."

"You need know nothing except that you are still in danger. And until this is no longer the case, you must stay on guard at all times. You must stay with me."

And in doing so, she'd turn into a blithering idiot. Not unless she could convince this obstinate prince that she needed some space. Needed to do something besides hang out in his house worrying about what would happen next.

Jamie remembered her mother saying that honey drew more flies than vinegar. Jamie turned on the honey, nice and thick. "Ben, I'm really, really going stir-crazy here. Can't we go somewhere? Anywhere? In the backyard? For a drive?"

"No."

She snapped her fingers. "I've got it. I know you have horses. I saw them out the window. We could go for a ride on your land. You do have riding horses, don't you?"

"Yes, but that is an insane idea. You would be a sitting target."

"How many acres do you own?"

"Fifteen thousand."

Jamie swallowed hard. And she'd thought her father's five-hundred-acre farm was more than enough to manage. "Okay, that's a lot of wide-open spaces. Couldn't we find one spot where we're hidden? I mean, with all that land, what are the chances he'll find us?"

"Too great for us to take."

She drew in a deep breath and called up all her reserves. "Look, Prince Ben, if you don't take me out of this house and on a horseback ride, I'll run away. I swear it."

"Then you would be a fool."

"I mean it. These walls are closing in on me. If you don't let me out of here, then the minute you turn your back, I'll be gone, and then where will you be?"

"The question is, where will *you* be? A victim?"

She hated his logic. Hated his unshakeable will. But she couldn't hate him, not when he was simply considering her safety. "Look, you'll either let me get out of here for a while, or you'll have to…have to…tie me up!"

The man had the nerve to smile. "Perhaps tying you up might be a pleasant option."

Turning, she headed for the door. She wasn't going to stick around for his mind games. "I'm going for a ride. If you want to come with me, fine. If you don't, that's fine, too. It's broad daylight. The man would be an idiot to come here when anyone could see him."

When she reached the door, Ben's hand came around her and slapped the solid wood surface. His warm breath ruffled her hair, glanced across her ear. "If you insist on doing this, I will accompany you on a horseback ride. And I will be by your side, trying to keep you safe. You'd best pray that I am able to do that."

Without thinking, she turned and circled her arms around his waist and gave him a solid squeeze. "Thank you. I really appreciate it."

He stepped away from her as if she'd slapped him instead of hugged him. "I will go change clothes."

"No!" She hadn't meant to sound so forceful, but she liked the thought of him riding with the wind whipping through his robes. Her fantasy come to life. She grabbed for a quick excuse. "It'll be dark soon. There's not time. Can't you manage with what you're wearing?"

He looked down, then back up at her. "Yes, I will manage with my clothing, but I must take something with me." He walked to the corner of the room, slipped open a bureau drawer and withdrew a metal object that glinted in the harsh overhead light. Jamie didn't have to see it to know it was a gun even though he quickly tucked it in the back of his slacks, underneath his robes.

Well, she would just have to put up with it in order to get her way and get out of here for a while. She hoped he didn't have any reason to use the gun.

Four

Ben silently cursed and called himself a fool while they rode through the near-barren terrain. He kept his eyes trained ahead as they passed through the oil fields, knowing each derrick could serve as a hiding place for Klimt. Even though Ben had kept men posted at the gate and several work hands riding the fence lines bordering the property, he still did not feel assured. His land was vast, and vulnerable in places. He did not have enough men in his employ to watch every area, every inch of barbed-wire fence where someone could easily slip underneath.

Yet he had allowed Jamie to talk him into this imprudent journey. But when she had looked at him with those innocent green eyes, he knew he would walk through fire to please her. And that weakness for her troubled him almost as much as the risk he now took. Angered him as well. He could not let down his guard.

With his free hand, he reached behind him and touched

the gun, but it afforded him little comfort. He prayed that Klimt would not have the resources, or the strength, to garner a weapon. Unless he stole one. That was a possibility Ben did not care to consider at the moment.

He glanced at Jamie and noted the brilliant smile on her face. Obviously she enjoyed her freedom. At least she rode in silence so that he might keep his ears tuned to the sounds. Blessedly, all he heard was the rush of the breeze through the coastal grass beneath them, the steady thump of horse hooves, and the occasional cow bawling in the distance.

She met his gaze and her smile melted into a frown. "Lighten up, Prince Ben," she said. "This isn't all bad."

"We must head back soon."

"Not yet," she said. "You promised me an hour."

An hour would be enough time for Klimt to find them. Why had he made such a promise? He knew why, but he did not care to examine his reasons. "The sun is going down, and it looks as though it might rain."

Jamie turned her face up to the sky. "Yeah. Smells like it, too. But it won't come for a while yet." She patted the leopard-spotted gelding's withers with one hand. "I was expecting you to own Arabians, not Appaloosas."

He allowed a brief smile. "They are well-suited to this country. My neighbor, Matthew Walker, has helped me establish a breeding program."

She gave the gelding another pat. "And what's this guy's name? I bet it's something exotic."

"Buck."

Her grin deepened, causing Ben's pulse to quicken. "Just Buck? That's funny."

"He was already named when I bought him."

She pointed at Ben's mount. "Let me guess. Barney?"

The sorrel stallion danced for a moment as if disturbed

by the insult. "He is called Fire, a part of his registered name."

"I guess that suits him." Jamie twitched in the saddle. "Can we lope for a minute? I'm tired of walking."

He'd expected her to ask sooner and had hoped for never. "We may trot, if you wish. I do not want you getting away from me for even a moment."

"Sure. Trot. Whatever." With that, she kicked the gelding into a gallop.

This time Ben verbalized his curses as he cued the stallion into a run. He managed to catch up to her, and, although he shouted at her to slow down, she did not heed his command.

Only when they approached the tree line surrounding a pond did she pull up. Ben stopped beside her, resisting the urge to tug her from the saddle to give her a healthy shake. Or a long kiss.

"This is beautiful," she said, her eyes wide. "It doesn't look like it belongs here."

Ben understood her admiration. He'd discovered the place the first time he had ridden the fields. The pond was framed by a few ancient live oaks that had survived the unforgiving elements. Yellow and lilac-colored wildflowers lined the banks that dipped down to the water's edge. An oasis of sorts—as close as he would get to one in this place called Texas.

Jamie continued to stare, silent, as if drinking in the sight. Ben studied her delicate profile, her soft lips, the column of her throat. He visually followed the path downward to her high round breasts. Heat coursed through him when he imagined kissing that same path, her flesh in his palms, naked and soft. His whole body seemed to lurch, reminding him that he did not dare give in to desire. Duty was of the utmost importance.

He cleared his throat to speak. "I come here often to think."

She turned her vibrant eyes to him. "I can see why. It's beautiful."

So was she, Ben thought. "Yes, it is."

With both hands on her hips, she leaned back in the saddle. "Boy, am I sore."

Without thought, Ben dismounted, led the stallion to a tree and tied him loosely to one branch. When he turned, he expected to see Jamie following suit, but she remained in the saddle. He walked to her and held out his arms to assist her. She braced her slender hands on his shoulder.

The act of helping her dismount should have been simple. But nothing about Jamie Morris was simple. Ben realized that fact when he slid her down the length of him. He had not meant to hold her so close. Perhaps he had, but not consciously. Regardless, she *was* close—so very close—that every place their bodies contacted, flames were left in the wake.

In his logical mind, he knew he should step back once her feet met solid ground. But he did not. Could not. She streaked her tongue across her bottom lip, fascinating him. Inviting him. He could not refuse such an invitation even though he knew to do so would be the most inadvisable thing he had done thus far.

Lowering his head, he captured her mouth, seizing the opportunity to sample what he had only imagined until now. Her lips parted, both surprising and delighting him. He slipped his tongue inside, softly, cautiously, not wanting to frighten her, or give her the excuse to pull away. Not until he had his fill of her, as if that were possible.

She readily accepted the play of his tongue and even engaged in some play of her own. Ben pulled her closer, but not close enough. His djellaba provided a barrier between them and for that he should be grateful. Had he been wearing his normal riding clothes, jeans and shirt, she would know how much this kiss was affecting him. How much he wanted her.

Jamie melted against Ben, relishing the feel of his strength, the spicy scent of his cologne. She pulled her hands from their resting place against his chest and slipped them beneath the robe so that she could span the width of his strong back. Feel the muscles she had admired on several occasions.

She heard a moan, but she wasn't sure who it had come from. Right now she felt like moaning all the way to Oklahoma and back. Never had anyone kissed her this way, with such a thorough gentleness, with only a flutter of his tongue in slow, fluid movements that made her feel like a bundle of hot, feminine yearning.

She was lost. Totally, completely disoriented, consumed by a raging need as unfamiliar to her as were the customs of this man now kissing her until she thought she wouldn't have a brain cell left in her head once he was done. She hoped he'd never be done.

Feeling incredibly brave, she slid her hands down his back, slowly, slowly, intending to rest them on his hips. Then she touched the cold hard steel of the gun.

Ben pulled away, looking as shaken as she felt. ''We must go.'' He walked to the stallion busy gnawing on a leaf from a low-hanging branch.

Shocked, Jamie couldn't move. Not an inch. It was as if the kiss had melted her feet, cementing them to the ground.

With the reins in one hand, Ben turned back to her and looked around. ''Where is Buck?''

To heck with Buck, Jamie thought. Where was her brain?

Glancing behind her, she noticed Buck wasn't there. He wasn't anywhere in sight.

"Buck's gone," she said, thankful she had found her voice.

Ben scowled at her. "Did you not tie him?"

"Of course not. You didn't give me a chance after you dragged me out of the saddle."

"I did not drag you. You came willingly."

"And you willingly put me in a lip lock."

"I do not remember you protesting."

Jamie didn't remember much of anything except the way he'd made her feel. "How did you expect me to say anything when you had your…your…"

"My mouth occupying yours? I believe you asked for my attention by opening your lips to mine. Is that not so?"

Jamie wasn't sure why they were playing this blame game. They were both to blame. And quite frankly, had she to do it all over again, she wouldn't change a thing. Even now, as he stared at her with those gray eyes the color of the near-night horizon, it would take only one move toward her, and he could have her again. All of her. Right here in the grass surrounded by flowers and weeds with the threats of a storm and a murderous man hanging over their heads.

She had really gone nuts. But it was Prince Ben's fault. He was driving her insane…. Crazy. Crazy for him.

And somehow, some way, she would have him again. She wanted more kisses. More of what she had never experienced in her twenty-two years. If she was in danger, she might not live to see twenty-three. Heck, life was a gamble. She could get struck by lightning, right here on the spot, because of her wicked thoughts. She refused to leave this earth without knowing what making love was all about. Without experiencing the heaven that existed between a man and a woman. And who better to teach her than the perfect prince named Ben.

* * *

Ben lay awake in his lonely bed for hours, wondering what he should do with Jamie Morris. What he could do about his weakness for a woman too hard to resist, even for a man who had spent his life practicing iron control. He could not afford to compromise her safety by again losing his head.

Rain drummed the tin roof above, a deluge that had come moments before they had arrived back at the ranch after they had finally located Buck. After the kiss. And Jamie, her skin dampened by the sudden downpour, hair wet, face innocent, had almost made him kiss her again. Instead, he had quickly retreated to safety, away from all that temptation.

A clap of thunder shook the walls, and he cursed the fact the storm muffled any suspicious noises coming from outside. His security system was the best money could buy, yet he still could not assure that a man as clever as Klimt—a man who had eluded them all—might not find a way to gain entry.

Aside from that prospect, he worried more about his feelings for Jamie. About his growing desire. Another threat to her well-being.

Perhaps he should make arrangements for Jamie to take up residence with another club member. But who? Certainly not his neighbor, Matt. He was planning to wed Lady Helena in the near future and they needed their time alone. Not Justin Webb and his wife, Winona. They had the responsibility of a child recently adopted by the couple. Aaron Black and his new bride, Pamela, awaited the birth of their firstborn. Which left only one member, retired air force colonel, Dakota Lewis, who had lived alone, estranged from his wife, for the past three years. As long as Ben had known the man, he had never heard Dakota mention being with another woman, perhaps because he still longed for his wife's company.

Yes, Ben could trust Dakota Lewis to keep Jamie safe. But what if he had been deprived of lovemaking so long that Jamie tempted him as well? Although Dakota was an honorable man, he was still a man.

Ben tightened his hold on the pillow in his arms, a poor substitute for a woman. For Jamie. He could not stand the thought of anyone touching her. Except for him. But he could not have her. Neither would he allow someone else to have her as long as she was in his care.

He was the only logical choice. The only one to protect her. He had made a vow, and he would not break it. He'd promised to keep her safe, and he would, even if that meant keeping his distance from her. He refused to let his desires override his common sense.

Rolling over, Ben flattened his face against the pillow. Did he really believe ignoring Jamie would be so easy? Did he truly think he could rein in his libido when every word she uttered, every smile she favored him with, made his heart gallop in his chest and his body come to life?

He must be strong. If he had to hide behind cool indifference, even anger, then he would. After all, it was for her sake—and his sanity.

He had no choice.

"Ben?"

At the soft sound of her voice, Ben's head snapped up. He could make out Jamie's small figure in the doorway. She was dressed in a short nightshirt that barely covered her thighs, her arms crossed over her breasts. His body again reacted to her presence even though she stood several feet away.

Between the steady rain and the fact he had been so lost

in his thoughts, he had not realized she had come in. How well would his inattention to his surroundings serve her?

Rising to a sitting position, he draped his legs over the edge of the bed. "Is there something wrong, Jamie?"

She took a few steps toward him. "I'm just feeling a little uneasy with the storm making such a racket outside. And I know it's really childish of me, but do you mind if I sleep in here with you?"

Yes, he minded, but not because he did not want her in his bed. Because he *did* want her in his bed. In his arms. Very unwise. Yet his inherent need to protect her, make her feel safe, kept him from refusing her request.

Moving to the far side of the bed, he raised the sheet and patted the mattress. "Come."

Quietly she moved to the bed and slipped in beside him. Ben turned onto his back close to the opposite edge, fearing even a brush of her smooth skin would cause him to lose control.

He glanced at her and saw that she, too, had turned on her back, studying the ceiling fan that whirred above them.

"Can I ask you something?" she said.

"Yes."

"When you kissed me in the pasture, did that mean anything to you?"

He wasn't prepared to discuss this now, not while she was so close. So soft and warm beside him, although they were separated by several inches. But he still sensed her heat, smelled her fragrance, longed for her touch.

He rubbed a hand over his bare chest, imagining her slender fingers there. "Jamie, please know that I find you very beautiful. Yet I cannot let what has happened between us interfere with the job I must do."

"Protecting me?"

"Yes."

"If that wasn't the case, do you think there might be more between us?"

Turning his head, he studied the outline of her delicate features set against the shadows. "Perhaps, but my life is complicated. I come from a culture that has certain expectations. Women are very different in my country. I am not accustomed to American beliefs."

"You mean you're not accustomed to women with a backbone?"

"Women who do not understand the way I have been raised," he corrected. "I cannot change who I am, or what I believe."

"I don't know, Ben. I think everyone has the capacity for change." She laced her hands together and stretched her arms above her head, pulling the nightshirt taut over her round breasts. Ben tried to avert his gaze but could not, and his whole body paid the price for his weakness.

"So I would guess that you see me as some wild, frivolous twenty-two-year-old girl who doesn't have the sense to take care of herself," she said, sarcasm in her tone.

He saw her as a woman any man would want, as he wanted her now. Young, yes, but with insight beyond her years. How could he explain this to her? How could he tell her that she was a precious gift that some man, some day, would be fortunate to claim? But not him.

He no longer knew where he fit in the grand scheme of things, even where he fit into his culture these days. He had changed, and change was not necessarily good. He was bound to his birthright, to honor his father's memory. If he no longer knew who he was, or what he wanted from life, then how could he involve her in his indecision, his inability to fit into either his culture or the one he had recently chosen?

He could only attempt to explain and hope she would

understand. "I believe you are a strong woman, Jamie. That is a good thing here in America. In my country, it is frowned upon. We are much more progressive than most, but our customs are slow to change. I have never been involved with an American woman for that reason."

"Never? Not even in college?"

"No, but I have not lived a celibate life, as you might believe."

She turned her face toward him. "Then who keeps you from being celibate?"

"Certain women in my country."

"Prostitutes?"

"No. Not in the sense you think. No money is involved."

"Mistresses?"

"Yes." He wanted to move off the disconcerting topic. He sounded like a dishonorable man when in reality it was an accepted part of his culture.

He looked at her once again. "Go to sleep or we will both be exhausted in the morning."

"One more thing." She turned on her side facing him, slipped one arm beneath the pillow and curled a delicate hand against her chest. Lightning flashed through the curtained window, illuminating her eyes. "My marriage to Payune. It wasn't my idea. It was my father's. I was trying to help him out. He needed the money for his farm. I just wanted you to know that. I would never marry a man I didn't love otherwise. And never again would I even consider such an archaic thing."

Ben internally flinched over her comment. Arranged marriages were common in his country. Still, he had often wondered why a beautiful young American woman such as Jamie had agreed to a marriage arrangement. Now he knew—an attempt to save her father from himself. His respect for her increased tenfold. "Where is your father?"

Her quiet sigh echoed in the room. "I don't know. He left before I was supposed to leave for Asterland. He has a problem with gambling and drinking. He's been that way ever since my mom died over a year ago. I've tried to help him, but he won't let me."

The sadness in her voice made Ben want to hold her, shelter her. He remembered how much his mother grieved his father's death at the hands of a dissident. How much she still grieved. And Ben had been too young to save his father from that fate and his mother from that grief. That was the reason he had vowed never to let harm come to anyone he cared about. But because of his mother's fortitude, she continued on with life as best she knew how. A testament to her strength.

"I am sorry about your mother," he said. "And your father's problems. Perhaps he will come around with time."

"Thanks. I hope so." She smiled. "What about your parents?"

"My mother is well in Amythra. My father died many years ago, when I was only a boy."

Jamie touched his arm. "I'm sorry, too, Ben. What happened to him?"

He truly did not want to discuss something so painful, but when Jamie looked at him expectantly, he had the strongest urge to tell her, reveal something he had never told another soul in America. "He was murdered at the hands of a extremist member of my father's opposition. As I said, I was very young. I was by his side when he was attacked outside the palace, yet I could do nothing to stop it."

"That's why, isn't it?" she said, her voice only a notch above a whisper.

"I do not know what you are asking."

"This whole protection thing. Your honor. It all has to do with the fact you couldn't save your dad."

How well she could read him. How well she seemed to know and understand his deepest secrets. "Yes. From that day forward, I vowed to defend and protect innocent people from those who have no regard for life."

She took his hand into hers and gave it a gentle squeeze. "If I haven't said it before, thanks for protecting me. I really do appreciate all you've done for me."

If only she knew how much more he wanted to do for her, including making love to her in ways that would make her cry out with pleasure. "You are welcome." He closed his eyes against her scrutiny. Guarded himself against sexual urges he could not ignore. Guarded himself against rising emotions he dared not claim.

He felt the mattress bend and sensed her turning over. Again he opened his eyes. He rolled to his side, facing her back, yet resisted the temptation to reach for her. Pull her against him. Lose himself in her.

"Ben, just one more question."

Hadn't she said that a moment ago? He hoped this would be the last request so he could try to sleep, if that were possible with her in his bed. "Yes?"

"Are you ever afraid?"

He was afraid now. Afraid of his growing feelings for this woman who seemed so strong, yet so vulnerable at times. Afraid that some day he would no longer be able to battle those feelings and would then give in to a yearning so intense, it almost consumed him. But he must resist, for many reasons.

"We must learn to face our fears," he said. "Otherwise, they will destroy us."

He heard her yawn again and prayed she was ready to sleep. "I think that's great advice. I'll remember it."

Silence stretched between them, and just when Ben thought she had fallen asleep, her silky voice broke the quiet. "Ben?"

More questions, he surmised. "Yes."

"Would you just hold me? I'd feel much better knowing you're close."

Against good judgment, Ben pulled her to him, much in the same way he had that first night. It took all his resolve not to turn her over into his arms, kiss her with all the emotion welling inside him. Prepare her body for him. Make love to her as if the dawn would never come.

The steady drone of spring rain kept time with his pounding heart. Drawing on his inner strength, he remained still, and waited until her breathing grew deep and he knew she slept.

Only then did he relax. Only then did he pull her closer, stroke her hair, savor her fragile body curled into his.

Only then did he whisper, "Jamie Morris, what have you done to me?"

Five

Jamie was just about at wit's end.

Two whole days and he'd barely talked to her. For two whole days he'd made it a point to avoid her, like she was a virus. Some contagious disease that threatened his health if he came near her.

Between mysterious meetings and business dealings, most conducted in the privacy of his home office, Ben had all but said she was a nuisance. An unwelcome guest.

Last night at dinner, she'd asked him to pass the salt. When he had, their fingers had touched, and he'd pulled away as if he'd been burned. The shaker had tumbled from her hands, spilling the salt. Out of habit, she'd tossed some of it over her shoulder for luck. Obviously that old wives' tale hadn't worked. Ben had only muttered an apology then gone back to reading the financial page of the paper. No luck there.

She'd resorted to telling jokes just to see if he would

laugh. Every now and then she'd managed a smile from him. She'd even told him about her plans, her ambitions, things she'd rarely told other people.

But she hadn't returned to his bed after he had told her that she wasn't his type. Well, big deal. That didn't mean he had to be rude. Or that she couldn't change his mind.

She'd had enough of his avoidance. Had enough of reading every magazine on the premises, cover to cover. Had enough of watching soap operas with Alima, the daily bedroom scenes only providing fuel for her dreams and the fire in her body Ben had stoked with his kiss. And, most importantly, she was fed up to here with Ben's continued withdrawal, his annoying silence.

Today she was determined to end it, even if she had to tie him up and force him to talk to her.

Jamie smiled at the thought of Ben shackled so she could do with him what she wanted, and what she wanted had nothing to do with talking.

You are a very bad girl, Jamie Morris. This time her mother's voice filtered into her conscience.

Jamie tuned out the scolding as she walked in to the living room, surprised to find Ben seated on the sofa instead of in his office, dressed in his cowboy clothes—torn jeans, ragged T-shirt, worn boots. He held a cordless phone propped between his jaw and his shoulder.

She couldn't decide whether she liked him as cowboy or prince. Both, actually. She liked him any way she could get him, which lately had been neither way.

His Arabic words, interspersed with English, floated around the room like cottonwood through spring fields. A soft lyrical sound, as if he spoke to a loved one. Maybe even a lover.

The jealousy hit Jamie full-force. Okay, so maybe he'd

lied about having a girlfriend from his country. Maybe he'd lied about a lot of things. It didn't matter.

She was with him now. She wanted his company. She wanted to give, and to receive all that he had to offer as a man. In doing so, she'd just have to protect her heart.

But first she had to convince him that she had certain needs he wasn't meeting. It had all started with that kiss, and she'd always been one to finish what she'd started.

Tiptoeing to the back of the sofa, she began kneading Ben's shoulders and the rigid muscles beneath her fingertips. He reached up and grasped her right hand but continued his conversation. She still had one unoccupied hand and didn't miss a beat with her massage.

"I must go now, Mother," he said, then clicked off the phone and tossed it onto the nearby end table.

Mother? So he hadn't been talking to a girlfriend after all. Jamie was filled with relief, and a strong determination to get his attention.

She dropped her hand and joined him on the sofa, leaving a comfortable distance. She didn't want to get too close—yet.

"That was your mother?" she asked.

Ben stared straight ahead. "Yes. She wants me to return to my country soon for a visit."

Jamie tried to fight back the disappointment. "Will you be leaving then?"

"No. I told her I could not because of unfinished business. She is not happy about it."

"I guess that's why you're so tense. You really do need to relax, Ben."

Only then did he look at her. "I will not relax until I see to it that Klimt is captured, and you are safe."

The name sounded familiar, but she couldn't hang a face on it. "Klimt? So that's the man who's after me?"

She could tell by the look in Ben's eyes that he regretted the slip. "Yes. Do you know him?"

Jamie chewed her bottom lip and searched her brain. "I remember the name. Is he from Asterland?"

"He was on the plane. He sustained injuries that until recently, kept him hospitalized. He escaped the morning you were almost run down."

"He was driving the car?"

"So we assume. And you have something he wants. Or he thinks you have."

Here we go again. That mysterious *something.* "What could I possibly have that he wants? I don't have anything anyone would want."

Ben locked into her gaze with those damnable gray eyes. "You are wrong. You have much that a man would want, although Klimt is after an object that has nothing to do with your feminine attributes."

At the moment, Jamie didn't give a darn what this mysterious man named Klimt wanted. She only knew what *she* wanted. Ben's kisses. Ben's hands on her. Anywhere. Everywhere.

She inched closer and brushed back a dark curl from his forehead. "Where's Alima?"

"At the market with J.D."

Jamie wanted to shout with glee. "So we're alone?"

His well-defined chest rose with the deep breath he drew. "Yes, we are alone."

"Good." Jamie moved closer, flush against his side. Oh, how she wished she had more experience in seducing a man. Her one boyfriend, Billy Joe Adams, had been all hands. After spending two years fending off his weekend groping, she'd eventually broken off their relationship with her virginity still intact. The boy had bored her to tears. All he wanted was a make-out session in the back seat of his father's revamped '56 Chevy. Jamie had wanted sweet words and gentle touches, not a tongue jockey with more moves than a seasoned wide receiver.

She wanted romance. A slow and easy seduction. Sweet, sensual words. Then and now. She wanted a man, not a boy.

She wanted Ben.

Considering the set of Ben's strong jaw and rigid frame, she doubted he could offer her what she wanted most. Correction. She doubted he *would* offer her what she wanted, needed. She had absolutely no doubt that he could handle it quite well, if he had a mind to.

Well, she'd just have to give it her best try, and see where things went from there.

Leaning closer to Ben, she traced a path along the tear at the thigh of his worn jeans. The dark hair on his legs tickled her fingertips, and tripped her pulse into a frantic rhythm. "Looks like you should've sent Alima for a new pair of jeans. These are threadbare."

"Stop."

"Stop what?" She smiled and sent her fingers back in motion, circling the bare flesh on his taut thigh. "I'm just making an observation."

"It is not your observation that is troubling me."

"What *is* troubling you, Prince Ben?" Her voice came out in a throaty whisper, taking her by surprise.

"We cannot do this, Jamie. What happened the other day cannot be repeated."

She lowered her voice to a teasing tone. "Why not? Don't you like the way I kiss?"

"I liked it too much."

Jamie was overcome by such power. A power that made her feel as if she could conquer the world, and maybe even Ben's resistance. "Then I don't see a problem. You won't let me leave the house, so why not spend the time getting to know each other better?''

She was beginning to get the hang of this, and she really, really liked being in control. ''You're a man, I'm a woman, and we both have certain needs.''

His expression didn't change, his face as hard as granite. As beautiful as polished stone. ''What needs do you have that are not being met? I have opened my home to you. If you wish something special to eat, I will be more than happy to tell Alima. If you wish me to get you some rental movies, I'll send one of my men. Tell me what you desire, and I will see to it that you have it.''

''I desire you, Ben. Just you.''

Letting her eyes drift shut, she braced for the impact of his lips on hers. Nothing.

Opening her eyes, she found him studying her, looking completely composed, but at least he hadn't moved away.

''You do not know what you are asking,'' he said, his voice deep and husky.

''I know exactly what I'm asking. Just a simple kiss, Ben.''

''Kisses are not simple, Jamie. You have no idea what will happen beyond that kiss. I cannot promise you that I will stop. Many nights I have imagined what it would be like to hold you, to take you beyond the limits you have only dreamed of.''

Now she felt totally breathless—and optimistic. ''I've dreamed of you, too. Every night for the past week.''

''But my duty to you prevents me from doing what I would very much like to do with you. To you.''

Jamie sat back and released a frustrated sigh. Regardless of his sexy words, the man was as immovable as a boulder. ''What does duty have to do with this? Or is it that I'm not good enough for you? Maybe you'd prefer a princess to a peon?''

He cupped her cheek with strong yet gentle fingers. ''You are probably too good for me.'' He stroked a thumb back and forth over her jaw. ''Fine as the most expensive silk. Pure. Too pure. Too innocent.''

''I'm not that innocent.'' Okay, so maybe Billy Joe had barely reached first base, but Jamie was primed for a home run in Ben's arms.

She covered Ben's hand with hers and slowly slid it downward—past her throat, beyond her collarbone, and laid it on her breast. ''Touch me, Ben. I need you to touch me. Kiss me. Prove to me that I'm good enough for your attention.''

Before Jamie could prepare, she found herself laid out on the sofa, underneath Ben's large lean body. And he was kissing her. Boy, was he kissing her! And with an urgency that sucked her breath from her lungs. He thrust his tongue between her lips in a slow, fluid rhythm, and she felt it everywhere.

Every muscle, nerve, private place ached for him. Ached for what she knew he could give her. He made her feel all woman, and he was definitely all man.

He broke the kiss and framed her face in his palms. ''Damn your beauty, your persistence,'' he murmured. ''I will give you what you need.''

Then he kissed her again and sent his hand underneath her knit shirt, cupping her breast through lace. She wanted more. So much more. She wasn't even sure what exactly *more* meant, but she'd know it if he gave it to her.

Slowly he lifted her shirt and released the front closure of her bra, then pushed the barrier aside. For a few moments he simply stared at her, then stared at his finger as he traced a path round and round her nipple. He muttered something in Arabic before raising his eyes to her. "You are exquisite."

For the first time in her life, Jamie actually felt exquisite.

Lowering his head, Ben sent brush-stroke kisses down the cleft of her breasts, homing in on her taut flesh with lips as soft as the featherbed she'd slept in since that first fateful morning.

Something deep within Jamie told her she should stop him. Not because she didn't want this. She simply didn't want to fall in love with him. She needed to be in control, and right now Ben was controlling every move with his wicked mouth and roving hands.

When he suckled her breast, she shuddered from the long-awaited sensations. He lifted his mouth and placed his lips to her ear. "Do you still want more, my Jamie? Have you needs that I have not yet met?"

"Yes." The word came out on a sigh.

"Then so be it."

Pulling her to face him, with agonizing slowness he traced a line down her sternum to her belly with a fingertip, pausing at the waistband of her shorts. He kept her locked into his gaze with hypnotic eyes. Then he kissed her again, all the while toying with the snap, but not opening it. Jamie thought she might actually scream at him, Just do it! Before she totally lost it, he undid the snap with one smooth move. She felt the track of the zipper as he lowered it and held her breath, waiting, wondering, hoping he wouldn't stop. She would die right on the spot if he didn't follow through.

He slipped his fingertips beneath the denim, drawing her shorts farther down her hips. But he didn't remove them completely. He didn't remove his hand, either. Instead, he worked his way beneath her panties, but went no farther.

A pleading sound bubbled up in her throat, brought about

by impatience, by desire, by a need so great she wasn't sure she had the strength to face it head-on.

Then he found her secrets with his strong fingers, steadily stroking her as if she were something fine. Something to be cherished. He whispered in her ear, more words she didn't understand. But she could imagine. She didn't have to imagine what he was doing to her; she could feel it.

She wound tighter and tighter as he centered on her tender flesh. Her body moved beneath his hand of its own accord. She couldn't seem to control it. She couldn't control anything at the moment. Not the moans from her mouth that Ben tried to silence with another kiss. Not the steady throb of desire and the building tension beneath his clever fingers. Not the climax that overtook her in strong breath-stealing swells, causing her body to pulse wildly out of control.

She whimpered like a child and clung to Ben in fear he would let her go. If he did, she would drift away to another dimension and might never come back again.

She drifted anyway. Shattered into shards of sheer feeling, as if she were made of crystal. Slowly she descended from heights she'd never dreamed she could achieve. Her respiration returned to her in slow degrees. Her eyes felt drugged, her body heavy, but it wasn't from Ben's weight. While she was recovering, he had gotten up from the couch and stood looking down at her.

She stared up at him, confused. He didn't seem at all pleased. In fact, he looked madder than a hen in a coop full of barking dogs. He might be furious at her, at himself, but he wasn't unaffected by what had happened between them. The proof was there for anyone to see, right below the waistband of his tattered jeans.

Jamie lowered her blouse and rose on bent elbows. "What's wrong?"

"You should not have to ask." He sounded irritated, his face hard as steel. A monument to an unbendable will.

"Ben, I'm—" She had no idea what to say. What could she say? *Ben, I'm really needing you. Ben, finish what you started. Ben, dammit, get back here right this instant.*

She reached out her arms to him. "Please, Ben. Don't leave me. Stay here with me." *Make love to me.*

He perched on the edge of the sofa and took her hand into his. "You do not understand, nor do I expect you to. I have broken a vow to myself not to let this happen between us. I do not wish to hurt you." He touched her cheek reverently. "But I fear I already have."

He rose slowly, looking pained and more than a little worried. Maybe even regretful.

Jamie grasped for the right words. "But—"

"There is nothing more to be said. I am sorry. I should not have done what I did."

Jamie's desire was replaced with frustration that he would just drive her over the edge then leave her so unsatisfied. Himself unsatisfied. "I'm glad you did do it, Ben. I have never felt that way before. Ever. And you're not going to make me feel guilty." She worked her shorts up her hips and sat up. "But if you're too stubborn to realize that I'm a big girl who knows her own mind *and* body, then you're hopeless."

A wry smile formed on his lips. "Then you do understand. I am hopeless, Jamie. Hopeless when I am around you. But it will not happen again. You can trust me on that."

He turned to leave without another word, and Jamie's heart sank to its lowest point in her life. But her determination grew to the length of a football field.

Prince Ben was in for a big surprise. He could try to fool her with his duty and honor, she wasn't falling for that. But was she falling for him?

Nope, she wasn't going to do that, either. She'd somehow convince him that the chemistry they shared was natural. And there would come a time when she would have him. All of him. Now she just had to come up with some plan to make him see it her way.

"Klimt's still around, Ben."

Ben strangled the phone's receiver, trying to digest Matthew Walker's words. "Are you certain?"

"Yeah. I rode out to Miller's place on Old Tackett Road. A man fitting Klimt's description stopped by there yesterday, according to Miller's foreman, Gus."

"What did he want?"

"To use the phone. Long-distance. He gave Gus some money after the call."

"Does he know who Klimt contacted?"

"Nope. Gus just said he spoke in some language he didn't understand. I suspect he probably called Payune."

"Then we should be able to prove it."

"I thought about that, but Justin says he doesn't want to get Winona in trouble, so we can't go asking for phone records yet. Not unless we want to involve the police. Right now we need to let Klimt make the next move and hope he'll lead us to the diamond, since he seems to be getting more desperate."

Which meant Jamie was in more danger, Ben thought. "I will tell my men to be exceedingly cautious."

"Yeah, you do that. And keep an eye on Jamie."

Ben had kept more than an eye on Jamie earlier, and the simple memory of how she had felt beneath his hands, looked in his arms, her cheeks tinged pink, her eyes soft with satisfaction, made him want to climb the walls now closing in on him. "I have been watching her closely and I will continue to do so. But I am not certain how long I will be able to convince her to stay here without telling her the whole truth."

"You've got to try. The less she knows, the better." Matt chuckled. "You'll just have to use every trick in the book to make her stay. I have faith in you."

Ben clenched his teeth to keep from cursing. If only Matt knew how little he deserved that faith. "I will do my best to convince her to stay, but she is not so easily swayed."

"Okay, if you say so."

"Anything more?"

"No. We're just keeping our ears to the ground, trying to find out more about the plot to overthrow Asterland's government. Looks like we might be forced to send Dakota Lewis over there after all."

Ben felt an overwhelming sense of relief that they had chosen Dakota for the mission. The last thing Ben needed was an assignment to Asterland when he had promised his mother a trip home in the near future. "He would be the natural choice."

"Yeah, but we're not ready to do it just yet. If we're lucky, Klimt will not only lead us to the diamond, he'll also lead us to Payune. With that proof, then maybe we won't have to do anything. We can just let the Asterland officials handle it themselves."

Ben prayed that would happen soon, and that Klimt would make a mistake and find himself caught before he again tried to get to Jamie. Then Jamie could return to her apartment, and Ben could go on with his life. His lonely life. "I must go now, Matt. Keep me informed on what you might learn of Klimt's whereabouts."

"You bet. And Ben, one more thing." Matt cleared his

throat. "No one here expects you to be a saint. Things happen. I found that out the hard way, but I don't regret meeting Helena. So if you and Jamie—"

"You have no worries there, *Sadíiq*. I do not intend anything to happen between us. I only intend to keep her safe." What a liar he had become.

Matt released a grating laugh. "Yeah. That's exactly what I said about Helena. And look at me now, just a few weeks away from getting hitched and damned glad about it."

Ben was happy for Matthew Walker, but he would not allow himself to fall into that same trap. Marriage was something he could not consider, especially with a woman like Jamie. An American woman full of life and optimism, a need for independence.

No, he would never be the man to make Jamie Morris happy. She was too innocent, no matter what she claimed. Too good for a man like him.

She'd just have to be his mistress.

That thought haunted Jamie all afternoon. Amazing that she could even think at all after what Ben had done to her, but since then, she'd been thinking as much about what he'd said several nights ago in his bed. About the women who served him. What did they have that Jamie obviously didn't? Maybe she should just come out and ask him? Like he'd really tell her.

As usual, he had retired to his office, and she to her lonely bedroom to mull over her situation. Refusing to read another magazine, she'd done a lot of mulling over the past few hours. Now she was determined to take action.

Tossing her book aside, Jamie went on a quest for information, in search of answers. And the one person other than Ben who might put to rest her curiosity was Alima.

She found the housekeeper two doors down in a guest room, wearing her usual plain gray cotton dress and white apron. The room was much the same as Jamie's, brightly colored and luxurious, but still empty by all rights, except for Alima who roosted on the edge of the bed, tuned in to her favorite soap opera on the small TV, a vacuum cleaner nearby. She was hiding out, Jamie suspected, since Ben was at home, squirreled away in his office. He hadn't been in the best mood lately.

Silently Jamie slipped onto the bed next to Alima. "So who's the good doctor pursuing today?"

Alima shot Jamie a sideways glance. "The *SaHafi*. Newspaper woman. The one who is, how do you say in English?"

"Loose?"

"Yes. She goes from one man to the next. Such terrible morals, that one has."

What a perfect lead-in. Maybe her luck was changing. "Speaking of loose women, tell about those in your country."

Alima turned her attention to Jamie, probably because of the commercial break. "I do not understand."

Jamie pulled her legs up and crossed them in front of her. "You know, *those* women. The mistresses. What do they do to please a man?"

Alima clucked her tongue. "A young girl such as you should not worry about these things."

Jamie raised her chin a notch. "I'll be twenty-three in two months, long past the need for a nursemaid. I'm sure as heck not worried. I'm just curious." For reasons she didn't dare reveal to Alima, Ben's surrogate mother. "Well, how do they please a man?"

Alima hid her face behind her hands for a moment before revealing a toothy smile. "There are many ways."

"How many?" Jamie cringed at how anxious she sounded.

"Countless. In my culture, these women learn to please by learning to be pleased, letting a man guide them."

Jamie's eyes widened. "How do the men learn?"

"At a very early age, the men are given a book that instructs them on how…" Alima looked away. "I should not be telling you these things."

Jamie touched her arm. "I won't tell anyone. What kind of book?"

"A book describing places on a woman's body, where to touch them to make them…" Alima averted her gaze, "…ready for the man."

Well that explained a lot about Ben. Just the thought of his touch made gooseflesh pop out all over Jamie's body. She had been more than ready. She still was. "So they have this book, they read it, and then they practice with these women?"

"Yes, that is the way."

"And do the women receive a book?"

"No. They must learn from the men."

That figured. Jamie wondered what happened to those poor women who had the misfortune of coming upon a rotten teacher. "So they learn by doing."

"Yes. They learn how to entice. How to undress to drive the man to—" Alima studied Jamie long and hard, wariness calling out from her near-black eyes. "I have said too much."

"No, really. Tell me more."

"Why do you ask me these questions?"

"I told you, I was just wondering."

"And you have no other reason?"

"Well, in case I might encounter a man from your cul—" Jamie had done it now. She could tell by the suspicion on Alima's face. "Not that I would anytime soon. I mean—not that there's any man around here that I would encounter in *that* way." Not that she wouldn't like to, and soon.

Alima sent her a knowing smile, taking Jamie by surprise. "Should you come upon this man, it is important you remember that he has been taught to remain in control. It is a strong woman who can break that control. Yet her strength lies in her willingness to quietly do his bidding."

"You mean to be passive." The word left a bitter taste in Jamie's mouth. She hated passive. She'd never viewed women as the weaker sex, at least not herself. But if being passive and restrained in her seduction would break Ben down, make him give her his all, then she'd do it. Once, and only once. Because if she didn't have him soon, she'd go nuts.

Standing, she put her best smile forward. "Thanks, Alima. You're the greatest."

"And you are a devious child." At least she said it with a grin, making Jamie feel a bit less guilty.

"Not devious, just interested." So maybe it was a teeny-weeny lie.

Alima went back to her TV program as Jamie headed to the door.

"Miss Morris."

Jamie turned to find Alima still staring at the tube. "It's Jamie. I prefer you call me that."

"As you wish, Jamie," she said, without turning around. "I have seen the book."

Jamie took a step forward. "You have?"

"I came upon it in the sheikh's library while dusting. It is placed next to the fourth book on the top shelf. Very pretty flowers on the cover. It is an English translation."

Jamie was now beyond shocked. She was flabbergasted. "Sounds like a very interesting read."

"I would not know. I do not read English well. There are many pictures, though."

Obviously Alima had sneaked a peek. "You certainly speak English very well."

"Prince Hasim is a good teacher of the American language. I believe he would be a fine teacher in many areas."

Jamie walked to the bed and gave Alima a hug. "Thank you."

Before Jamie released her, Alima patted her hand and said, "Be cautious, my child. A woman who strives to lose her innocence may lose her heart to one who cannot give his in return."

"Thanks. I'll remember that."

Jamie left the room with Alima's cautions echoing in her brain. If she followed through with her plan, would she be in danger of losing her heart to the sheikh, a man who obviously had no interest in love?

No, she would not allow that. If she could keep from it. She couldn't consider that now. At the moment she needed to find the book, then find a way to practice passive.

Six

Jamie really wanted to tear his clothes off.

Not an appropriate thing to do considering they were sitting at the dinner table with Alima nearby in the kitchen. But having spent the afternoon reading "the book," complete with colored illustrations, the images still danced around in her head—images of Ben and lovemaking. Although the book was tastefully written, the pictures and text left nothing to the imagination. Especially Jamie's imagination, which at the moment was working overtime.

Alima scurried into the dining room with a platter full of fragrant meat, vegetables and pastries.

"What is the occasion, Alima?" Ben asked, the first words he'd spoken since they'd sat down.

She set the platter in front of Jamie and began piling the fare onto Jamie's plate. "I do not understand."

"First you bring us the oyster stew, and now this." He gestured toward the platter. "You normally do not serve *máaza* unless it is a special event. And if you do not quit filling Miss Morris's plate, there will be none left for me.''

Alima nodded and began serving Ben his food. ''It is in honor of our guest.'' She raised her eyes to Jamie who saw a helping of amusement there as big as the mountain of food on her plate.

''I see.'' Ben raised his glass of wine and tipped it toward Jamie. ''To our guest.''

Jamie clinked her own glass against his in a toast. ''And to my very accommodating host.'' Who she hoped would be much more accommodating as the evening progressed.

Sipping the wine slowly, Ben regarded her with his steel-colored eyes, but she couldn't begin to read what he was thinking. ''Is there anything else you wish from Alima?''

''Not that I can think of. I have everything I need.'' *At least from Alima.*

Ben dismissed the housekeeper with a sweep of his hand and the woman quickly left. He took his gaze from Jamie and centered it on the wineglass. ''Did you have a pleasant day?''

Jamie wanted to laugh. He had no idea how pleasant her day had been. He should, considering the episode on the couch. ''It was okay. After you ran off, it was just the usual, watching a little TV, that sort of thing.'' *Thinking about what you did to me on the sofa. Reading an Arabian sex manual.*

''I have made arrangements with your landlord,'' he said without looking at her. ''He has agreed to keep your apartment available for you. I have hired several men to watch over it should Klimt happen to return.''

''Great.'' She didn't want to think about her apartment or the fact that a maniac was still on the loose. All she could consider was Ben sitting before her, dressed in his

casual clothes, his jaw shaded with evening whiskers, looking much too sexy to ignore.

Time for plan A, Jamie decided. Getting Ben alone. "After dinner, do you mind if we talk a while before I go to
bed?"

He raised his eyes from the glass to her. "Something
important?"

"Yes, I guess you could say that." Important to her,
anyway.

"Shall we discuss it now?"

"No. Later. After Alima goes to bed."

"As you wish. I have something important to discuss
with you as well."

Did she dare hope that he'd changed his mind? Could
he possibly want to show her that he did want her? How
silly for her to consider that. Nothing had changed in a
matter of hours, at least not with Ben and his almighty
conviction. Obviously she had her work cut out for her
tonight.

After they had dined in silence, Alima cleared the plates
while Jamie joined Ben in the living room. This time he
took the huge leather lounge chair, leaving Jamie alone on
the nearby sofa.

He might as well have erected a brick wall, Jamie
thought. This was going to be harder than she'd imagined.

A few minutes of awkward silence passed before she
asked, "What did you want to discuss with me?"

Ben rubbed large fingertips up and down the arm of the
chair, bringing to mind his touch, the way he had reduced
her into a pool of need with his sturdy fingers. "Klimt has
been seen in this vicinity."

Jamie's eyes snapped up from Ben's hands to meet his
glance. "How close was he?"

"At the ranch adjacent to Matthew Walker's, which is next to mine."

Too close for Jamie's comfort. "Did someone call the police?"

"I told you that we cannot involve the police. If we do, Klimt will not lead us to what we're looking for."

"Oh. The *something*."

"Yes, and I have made sure my men are on guard."

An idea came to her, sharp and clear even if she hadn't planned it. "I know I'd feel much better with you in my room."

"Perhaps that would be a good idea."

This was too easy. "I'd appreciate it."

"I will move the chair by the window."

He wanted to sleep in the *chair?* A chair could prove to be a challenge. Did they mention chairs in the book? "Okay. If that's what you want. But we have slept together before and—"

Ben's frown stopped Jamie in mid sentence. She looked from Ben to find Alima standing only a few feet away.

"If you do not need me, I shall retire for the evening," Alima said.

Ben checked his watch. "It is only 8:00 p.m. Are you not feeling well?"

Alima kneaded her hands, looking a bit flustered. "No, Prince Hasim, I am simply tired. I shall go to my room immediately." She turned to Jamie. "Good evening, Miss Morris. Should you require anything through the night, please do not hesitate to summon me. But remember that I go to sleep with my music playing in my ears, so I do not hear a sound until I remove my ear phones much later."

With that, she turned and left the room. Left Jamie with her mouth gaping open and a smile that wanted to surface. Alima proved to Jamie once again that she was a wise woman. She knew exactly what Jamie intended for Ben, and she had all but given her permission.

Jamie almost laughed at Alima's obvious matchmaking attempts, but all humor died when she saw Ben's serious gaze. "Do you know what is wrong with her?" he asked.

"Wrong? No. She looks fine to me." Time for a subject change. "As I was saying, Ben, you don't have to sleep in the chair. You can stay on your side of the bed, and I'll stay on mine." Which didn't mean she couldn't accidentally roll his way, catching him off guard.

"That would not be advisable."

Darn his stubbornness. "You don't have to worry about me attacking you in your sleep." She would make sure he was still awake before she made her move.

"I am not worried about you." His dark eyes burned into her, causing Jamie to shiver. "It would be best if I keep my distance."

Jamie shrugged and pretended indifference. Time to institute plan B. "Suit yourself. But before we continue this conversation, I want to take a quick shower and get ready for bed. Then we can talk some more."

"All right. I shall do the same, and I will be waiting here for you when you return from your bath."

They stood at the same time and although they remained several feet apart, tension hung thick in the air. Before Jamie gave everything over to impulse, she turned and headed to the bathroom.

Once inside, she slipped off her clothes and released a ragged breath. Every inch of her body responded when she thought about what she planned to do next. Would she really have the courage to seduce him again? Would he stop her, or worse still, turn away? And if she were successful, would she be strong enough to resist the emotional entanglement already threatening her heart?

No doubt about it, with each day that passed came another reason to like him. His honor and honesty. His overt sensuality. Two days ago, she'd managed to unveil more of the man beneath the prince, and she admired what she had discovered—a born protector with a will as strong as reinforced steel and a vulnerability he tried to hide behind a tough facade. But she was beginning to see that vulnerability—that chink in his armor—more and more. She wanted to know everything about the man she had come to admire. The man she could easily love.

She shook her head, trying to shake the cobwebs from her common sense. *No, no, no!* She refused to fall in love with him. Ever.

Just short of entering the shower, she caught sight of the vanity counter and halted. Laid out next to the sink was a gown much like the one she'd worn the first day of her arrival. But this one was a pale peach color and twice as sheer. Next to it sat a bottle of pink-tinted liquid.

Making her way to the sink, Jamie picked up the bottle. She flipped open the lid and sniffed, then placed a few drops in her palm. Oil. Strawberry-scented oil. She held the bottle up and studied the unreadable label. Unreadable to someone who didn't know a scrap of Arabic.

Alima the Headphoned Housekeeper playing matchmaker.

The woman had made herself Jamie's partner in crime. Who else would leave instruments of seduction? Certainly not Ben. He wouldn't even agree to get in bed with her, much less provide her with a naughty nightie and a bottle of fruity oil.

This time Jamie did laugh, allowing her mirth to bubble over. She felt exhilarated, alive and prepared for whatever challenge Ben had in store for her.

Poor Ben. He had no idea what she intended, but he would, and soon. Very soon.

Ben had no idea what Jamie Morris was up to, but he had his suspicions. Every move she had made, every word she had spoken, made him recognize how very hard she would be to resist. A cold shower had done nothing to squelch his desire for her, not that he believed it would, even though many extolled the virtues of icy water in enabling a man to forget his lust. Rubbish, as his mother would say.

Settling back on the couch, Ben waited for Jamie, afraid to face her, excited by that prospect. He silently prayed she would dress appropriately and not descend upon him wearing the nightshirt that barely disguised her feminine charms.

A few moments later, Ben sighed with relief, thankful that Jamie had reentered the room wearing a heavy robe. Yet, even encased in red velvet, he could still imagine the woman beneath. Every curve, every crevice. The thoughts would surely be the death of him.

Averting his gaze from the gaping bodice of the robe, he said, "I presume you enjoyed your bath since you have been gone for almost an hour."

Smiling, she continued to stand, one hand hidden away in the robe's pocket. "Yes, it was nice. I enjoy a long bath. It clears the mind and relaxes the body, so to speak." She took a few steps forward until she was standing above him. "How was yours?"

Every blessed thought left his brain when soft feminine smells filtered into his nostrils. "How was my what?"

"Your shower. I assume you took one since your hair's wet. Although I wonder, since you still have on your jeans."

Jeans that grew tighter with each coy look she sent him.

"Yes, I showered. I felt it appropriate that I remain in most of my clothes." And he cursed the fact he had not put on his shirt. Perhaps his subconscious was setting him up to fail. Or testing his strength.

With a devilish smile, Jamie slipped the robe from her shoulders, revealing everything to him through the film of a sheer gown—her round luscious breasts, the shadow between her thighs, the curve of her hips. But before he had time to savor the sight, she was on her knees before him, staring up at him, her emerald eyes alight with desire. He had seen that look earlier, and there was no mistaking it now.

"Jamie," he said, caution in his tone. "I beg you to consider what you are about to do."

She ran a slender finger up his thigh. "Relax, will you? I just thought you looked a little worried during dinner. A little uptight. I'm here to help. Your wish is my command."

He wished she would leave him to his misery. How could he relax when she was so very close, only partially dressed, looking like temptation incarnate? "I am fine," he said, his jaw tight, his frame rigid, his belly clenched, belying his conviction.

"Yeah, right. And I'm Marilyn Monroe."

Inching forward on her knees, Jamie slid both palms up his thighs and parted his legs, then moved between them. Ben clawed his way back to reality. He must stop her now, before he could not.

"Jamie, I do not think—"

She slid her hands further up his thighs and brushed a fingertip over his groin. "For once, would you just stop thinking, Ben? Just try to feel. Enjoy the moment."

Rising farther up on her knees, she feathered kisses along his ear, his neck, then lower still across his bare chest. Ben grasped the sides of her head, intending to pull her away.

But as if he had lost his will to fight, he followed her movements as she laved her tongue across his nipple, much in the same way he had done to her earlier that afternoon.

Coherent thought ceased for a time until Ben's self-control took over. He lifted her face. "Jamie, we have been through this. We cannot do this."

She smiled. "There's no 'we' involved at the moment. I'm doing this. Just me, and all you have to do is sit back and take pleasure in it. That's all I'm asking of you."

Dipping her hand into the pocket of the robe, she withdrew a bottle of liquid and placed several small drops in her palm, then tossed the bottle aside. With long slender fingers, she worked the oil up over his shoulders, across his chest to his abdomen, drawn tight against the sensual assault. All the while Ben grasped the arms of the chair to keep from touching her. Keep from grabbing her up and kissing the life out of her. Keep from carrying her to his bed.

If she wanted to play this game, he would let her for the time being. As long as he remembered not to let things progress beyond the point of no return. Yet, at the moment, the feel of her delicate hands stroking his body robbed him of his resolve to stop her.

"Ben," she whispered against his belly, then washed her tongue in his navel.

Give me strength.

His plea went unheeded as Jamie released the snap on his jeans. His erection strained against the denim and he longed for the freedom that only Jamie could give him. But at what cost?

Before he could consider what she was doing, she had his fly completely open. He managed a smile when she looked up at him, shock in her expression. Perhaps her fear would stop her as nothing he could say would.

Her eyes widened. "You don't have anything on underneath these, do you?"

"I find that unnecessary under the circumstance, do you not agree?"

"Oh." She looked down again as if uncertain what to do next.

If she had never experienced the sight of a man aroused, perhaps that would convince her she was playing with fire. That consideration, and the fact Ben could no longer stand the torment, led him to slip the denim down his hips, revealing everything to her eyes. Blessed freedom at last.

Jamie continued to stare and repeated, "Oh."

"Does my body frighten you, Jamie?"

She shook her head and ran a fragile finger down the length of his shaft, sending tremors coursing throughout his entire being. She touched him again, this time with oil-slick palms, tentatively at first, then more boldly. She had regained her composure while Ben's slipped farther away with every touch.

Without removing her hands, she raised her eyes to him and said, "Does this please you, Sheikh Rassad?"

He could not remember the last time he had been so pleased, or so achingly hard from wanting a woman. "Yes. It pleases me very much."

"What else would please you?"

He clung to his last shred of will. "For you to stop this torture before it is too late."

"I don't want to stop. I want to return the favor for what you did for me earlier today."

Exactly what he feared. "That is not necessary."

"Oh, I think it is."

Jamie Morris was not an innocent, that much Ben decided before his thoughts began to slip away. Considering the way she touched him, caressed him with fine silken strokes, obviously someone had taught her well, and he hated that someone, although he had no idea who he might be. Hated him because he had been the first man to touch Jamie, and Ben had mistakenly assumed he would be her first.

At the moment, Ben could not consider her with another man, doing this to another man. He was on the brink of totally losing control, but he would not allow it to happen here. And when she lowered her head as if to take him into her mouth, resistance was no longer an option.

With an animal groan, he moved her aside and stood to step out of his jeans, unable to contain his overpowering desire for her. Damn the consequences. He needed to have her—be inside her—as much as he needed air to breathe.

She gave a little squeak of protest when he scooped her up in his arms. "Ben, I'm not done yet."

"Oh yes, you are most certainly done," he whispered as he passed through the living room toward the other side of the house. Toward his bed and the promise of pleasure. Toward the point of no return. "But I am only beginning."

Jamie now realized what it truly meant to be swept away by an Arabian knight. Engulfed in Ben's strong arms and heady male essence, she rested against his hair-covered chest where the thrum of his heart beat out an erratic rhythm against her cheek.

She was breathless, thrilled and a tiny bit afraid of what she had unleashed in Ben.

He entered the room and kicked the door closed behind them, then brought her down on the bed in his arms. Ben's arousal pressed against her belly, robbing her of her voice. Muted light filtered in from the adjoining bathroom, allowing her to make out the fire in his dark eyes.

"Do you know what you have done, Jamie?" he said.

She had her suspicions. "I've finally managed to see your bedroom again." A weak attempt at humor, Jamie decided, especially when she noticed Ben wasn't smiling.

He pushed the hair from her forehead and framed her face in his palms. "I believe you underestimate your power. Tell me now, while you still have the opportunity, if you wish to go forward. If you are uncertain, I will let you leave. But if you do not stop me, then I promise I will see this through."

Jamie didn't hesitate for a moment. "I want this, Ben. I have for a while now."

"Then it is done."

He kissed her thoroughly, hurling a spear of heat that settled in intimate places craving his touch. His tongue danced against hers, moving in and out between her parted lips. He teased and tempted her until she shifted restlessly beneath him.

Breaking the kiss, he pulled her up and worked the gown up and over her head. His expression was almost frightening in its intensity. She wasn't necessarily afraid of him, but she was more than a bit apprehensive over the intense desire sparking in his eyes—worried over whether or not she would please him. What did she know about the art of lovemaking? Not nearly enough.

His features softened when he touched her cheek, his gaze roaming over her face, seeking, searching. If he expected to find some hesitancy there, he wouldn't. She was determined not to let him see anything but longing.

"My Jamie," he whispered as he touched his lips to her temple, her cheek, her jaw. Then he sent his hands on a mission down her body, lingering at her breasts, fondling her until she shook with the force of her need.

"You tremble," he said. "Are you afraid?"

"No."

"Do you desire more?"

To say no would be one whopper of a lie, regardless of her concern. "Yes."

"Then lie back. Let me show you all the ways a man pleasures a woman."

Lying down sounded like a great idea to Jamie. She felt as weak as a starved woman. In some ways she was starving—for Ben's undivided attention. And she was getting it. Boy, was she getting it. His lips drifted down her neck then closed over her nipple. Her back arched as if it had a mind of its own, thrusting her chest upward, giving Ben better access. Slipping his hands underneath her back, Ben paid equal attention to both her breasts, and it was all she could do not to cry out from the pleasure.

Jamie couldn't seem to stop shaking. She wasn't the least bit cold, either. In fact, she was hot. So hot she could melt the mattress.

Ben sat up and straddled her thighs, then took a nearby pillow, placing it under her hips. He brought her hands up to his face and touched his lips to each of her palms. "I want to kiss you," he said.

Jamie reached up to cup his jaw in her hands and tried to draw him back to her eager mouth. He wouldn't budge.

"A more intimate kiss," he said. "I do not want you to be afraid."

She was more excited than fearful. Maybe a little of both. Did he really mean what she thought he meant? Only one way to find out. "Okay." Her voice sounded small compared to Ben's.

Then he lowered his head to nuzzle his face between her thighs, and she knew exactly what he had meant. The promise of a kiss like none she had ever known.

At the first intimate contact of his tongue on her vulnerable spot, Jamie's hips rose off the pillow.

"Be still," he said, his voice a gentle command.

Be still? How could she be still when her body wouldn't let her? Somehow she managed not to move too much, even when he delved deeper, using his tongue, his lips, to drive her to the threshold of the ultimate insanity.

She couldn't stifle the sounds leaving her mouth, sounds as unfamiliar to her as this act he performed with such tender persuasion. Lights flashed behind her closed lids. Sensations overtook her, not unlike those he'd created with his touch earlier that day, but more intense. He increased the pressure of his expert mouth until Jamie thought she might actually scream. Then the sensations overtook her as the pressure began to build and build, driving her toward release.

Jamie was totally captive to Ben's will as he continued with his kiss. Nothing could prepare her for the ensuing climax. Not a book. Not her imagination. Nothing.

The moan left her mouth regardless of her efforts to stop it. It was as if she left her body for a time, yet she'd never been so aware of every wonderful sensation. She didn't want it to end, but it did, leaving behind a slow dissolving heat and a sense of total euphoria.

Opening her eyes, she met Ben's gaze and his crooked smile. Male pride, plain and simple. Some things were inherent in every man, regardless of their background.

"Did that bring you pleasure, Jamie?" he asked in that slow-burn voice that made her want to moan some more.

"Isn't it obvious?"

"Good. But I am not yet finished."

The man had the nerve to touch her *there* again, and again she didn't have the strength to fight the onslaught of feelings, nor did she want to. But before she toppled over the edge, he came back to her. She groaned in protest.

"Patience." His smile came full-force. "It is not over yet."

With that he pulled her closer to him. She felt the nudge of his erection, and braced her hands on his shoulders. She closed her eyes tightly.

As he began to enter her, he met the resistance Jamie knew would come with her first time. He suddenly stopped trying, and she kept her eyes closed against his scrutiny although she could feel his gaze on her.

"Jamie, please do not tell me—"

"Okay, I won't."

"Look at me." His tone demanded she comply, forcing her eyes open. "Are you a virgin?"

"As a matter of fact…yes."

He turned his face upward and released a heavy sigh. "Why did you not tell me?"

"You didn't ask."

He started to pull away, but she wouldn't let him. "You finish this, Ben. I swear if you don't, I'll never forgive you."

He studied her for another long moment. "Perhaps I'll never forgive myself for abandoning good sense, but logic be damned. If this is what you wish, so be it. I cannot resist you." With one hard thrust, he filled her completely.

Jamie winced and held her breath. Ben stilled against her, allowing her body time to adjust to his intrusion.

"You tempt me to hurry," he whispered. "You feel so good surrounding me. Like velvet."

"Then hurry. Please."

It wasn't the pain that had her wanting him to get on with it. The sheer power of Ben's possession filled her with impatience. The pain had all but subsided, and in its place came a need so great she couldn't even begin to understand it.

He moved slowly, withdrawing a bit, then sinking deeper inside her. "Am I hurting you?" he asked.

"No. Not anymore."

His next move made her grit her teeth, not with pain but with intense pleasure.

"Did you feel that?" he asked.

Heavens, did she feel it! "What did you do?"

"I am searching for a special place."

He'd found it all right. Again. Then his hands seemed to be everywhere as he thrust inside her. He touched her in places she didn't know existed. With tenderness he took her higher, whispering words of praise. "My Jamie," he repeated over and over, and for a moment she truly believed she was his. He had branded her with his body, and now claimed her heart in spite of her caution.

Soon she couldn't think as she again embarked on another journey to sweet freedom. She didn't know exactly how he was managing to draw another climax from her, but he was, and she really didn't care how he'd done it. She only cared about how he felt in her arms, his power, his strength, his sensuality that called out to the deepest recesses of her soul.

This time, when she reached the summit, she cried out his name. And her name left Ben's lips, too, before he shuddered then stilled against her.

Pure joy had long been absent from Jamie's life, but now that joy had returned in Ben's arms. She wanted to sing. She wanted to cry. She simply held on to him, stroked his thick dark hair, kissed his solid shoulder, took to memory everything he had given her. Try as she might, she couldn't take back her heart. He possessed it now, just as he'd possessed her body.

Alima's warning came back to her.

A woman who strives to lose her innocence may lose her heart to one who cannot give his in return.

Jamie called herself ten kinds of fool. She had fallen in love with him—a man who couldn't love her in return.

Seven

Ben had never been so satisfied in his life. Jamie's fragile body fit perfectly to his, as if they were truly one. They had been one, at least for a few blessed moments.

Fearing he was crushing her with his weight, he moved to his side and regretfully slipped from her body. When he saw the glimmer of tears in her eyes, only then did he realize what he had done. She had told him she wanted this, but had she really known her own mind?

No. And he had acted on impulse, stolen her innocence. He had never bedded a virgin before, for many valid reasons, the most important being honor. He had learned during his upbringing that a man did not take something so precious without answering for his decision. His honor was now at stake, and only one option remained.

"We shall be married."

Jamie sat up in a rush and pushed back against the headboard. "Excuse me?"

Ben sat up too, resting his arms on bent knees. "We must marry now. I have taken your virginity, and it is only right."

Her eyes widened. "Now just a cotton-pickin' minute, Ben Rassad. In case you haven't noticed, this is a new century, and you're in America. That old virginity-marriage clause is no longer in effect."

Leaning over, he flipped on the bedside lamp. Seeing Jamie naked and flushed stirred his body to life again. He grasped the bed sheets and flung them across her body, covering all that temptation.

"I have told you I cannot change the way I believe," he said. "And I believe I am now obligated to marry you."

"Obligated?" Jamie clasped and unclasped a fistful of the sheet, a storm gathering in her green eyes. "I don't marry out of obligation."

"Are you certain? If I recall, you almost married Payune for that very reason."

"You jerk."

Ben wanted to take back his callous words. He wanted to tell her more, admit that he cared for her deeply. He did not know if what he felt was love, but he imagined it could be if given time. Yet he didn't dare admit that until he was certain. His honor also bound him to tell the truth.

Her eyes clouded with unshed tears, and he cursed the fact he had put them there. But what could he say to convince her that his intentions were honorable? He would simply have to try. "I would see to your every need. I would make you my princess. I would give you everything you desire—"

"Except love." She impaled him with her troubled green eyes. "But that's okay. I don't want your love. I don't need your love. I don't need anything, or anyone."

"Then you will not consider my proposal?"

"Not on your life. People don't have to marry this day and time because they have sex."

"Make love."

"In the absence of love, it's sex," she said adamantly. "I mean, women don't *have* to marry even if they get pregnant." Suddenly Jamie's eyes grew large. "Oh my gosh. *Pregnant.*"

The word echoed in Ben's ears. "Jamie, are you not protected against pregnancy?"

"How could I be? You've kept me cooped up in this house. And besides, it's your responsibility, too."

Ben had to admit he should have seen to that responsibility, but the thought had not entered his mind. This was not something he normally concerned himself with. "The women I have known in my country see to their protection."

Jamie narrowed her eyes and glared at him. "Well, great. We're not in your country, and I'm not one of *those* women. Haven't you heard of condoms?"

"Yes. Of course. I wrongly assumed you might be taking the birth control pill. You were very prepared in your seduction, so why would I not believe you would be prepared to protect yourself against pregnancy?"

"Because I'm an idiot." Jamie clutched the pillow to her chest. "This is just all I need."

All the energy seeping from him, Ben stretched out and rolled to face her. "Could you be with child?"

She worried her bottom lip. "I guess it's possible, but it was only once. Surely that counts for something. I mean, who gets pregnant their first time?"

He sought her gaze. "Many, I imagine, and all the more reason for us to wed. If you are carrying my child, you will be carrying another heir to my father's kingdom." And the son or daughter Ben had always secretly wished for, but never considered a possibility.

Jamie pushed off the bed, retrieved her gown from the floor, and slipped it back on. "I have no intention of marrying someone because I might be pregnant. And I sure as heck am not going to marry someone because I happened to lose my virginity to them during a fit of insanity." She spun around and headed toward the door.

He sat up quickly. "Jamie, where are you going?"

She paused with her hand on the knob, her back turned to him. "To my room."

He did not dare let her leave. Tonight he wanted her with him, for many reasons, the first being that he needed to ensure her safety. The second was much more selfish. He craved her nearness, wanted her curled up next to him until the dawn. Wanted to make love to her again and again, until they were both too exhausted to consider anything but each other.

Slipping from the bed, he caught the door before she could open it and leave. Both hands braced against the wooden surface on either side, he leaned into her and rested his face against the back of her head, drawing in the sweet smell of her damp hair. "Stay with me."

"Why?" she asked without turning around.

"I want you in my bed."

"You've already had me in your bed. Three times, last count."

"Yes, but tonight was different."

"You can say that again. And right now I wish I could take tonight back. I regret I've been so careless."

Ben had no regrets about making love to her. He only regretted that he could not give her what she needed, a promise of love. He had built armor around his emotions

for so long, he did not know if he could rid himself of it.
But perhaps he could try, if she would give him the chance.

He ran his fingertips over her hip, then grasped her waist
to pull her to him. "I need to keep you nearby. Keep you
in my arms. Keep you safe."

Jamie tried to ignore his low, whispery words, the feel
of his arousal pressed against her bottom. She couldn't, but
that didn't mean she had to do what he was asking. She
longed to stay with him all night, but feared that by doing
so, she'd give in to his demands and agree to his proposal.
Agree to anything, for that matter. She refused to do that,
give up her control. She wouldn't marry a man who didn't
love her; she'd made that vow after Payune had called off
their arranged marriage. She couldn't commit to a stranger.

Ben was no longer a stranger, but he didn't love her.
Yes, he might desire her, but that wasn't enough to build
a marriage on. She wanted love. She wanted *him* to love
her. Stupid, senseless fantasies.

Jamie didn't dare turn around. Just one look in his dark
eyes would have her melting like gooey fudge all over the
carpeted floor. "I'm going to my room now. I need some
space. Time to think."

"To think about what I have proposed?"

"No. I need to think about where I can go to get away
from here. Away from you."

"You cannot leave until—"

"I know. Until you find this Klimt. I can find somewhere
else to go. I know Lady Helena. She's right next door with
your neighbor, Matt. I imagine she'll let me hang out there
for the time being."

Ben pushed away from her, muttering in Arabic with a
severity she'd never before witnessed. "That will not be
necessary. You may remain here, and I will give you your

peace. I shall not touch you again. And damn you for what you have done to me.''

She heard the slamming of the bathroom door behind her, and moved into the hallway on rubber legs. The tears came then, slow and steady, falling down her chin and onto the floor. She welcomed them as punishment for exposing her tender heart to Ben. It wasn't his fault; it was hers. She had shamelessly seduced him, not once thinking about the consequences. Not once realizing that something as intimate as making love could be so emotionally overwhelming. Ben was right, it wasn't simple, giving everything to someone.

Now he wanted to do the honorable thing and marry her. Make her his princess. No matter how much she cared for him, she couldn't do that. Not unless he said the words she needed to hear—*I love you.*

Ben braced his hands on the sink and lowered his head. Turning on the faucet, he splashed cold water on his face, yet it did nothing to relieve the inferno raging inside him, or the terrible ache in his heart.

Jamie had given him her body without hesitation, yet she refused to be totally his. He could not blame her. She deserved a man who could commit all his heart. A man who knew where he fit into this world. He was not that man. Still, deep inside he wondered if she could change him. Show him this elusive emotion known as love. Love between a man and a woman.

He loved and respected his mother and father as a son should, but he was uncertain he could ever let down his guard and bare his soul completely to a woman, although tonight he had come closer than he ever had before. Yet Jamie would not marry him, or so she said.

What if she now carried his child? He must make her

understand the importance of their union. But should she finally agree to the marriage, would he be doing her a disservice by thrusting her into a culture intolerant of strength in a woman? His mother had survived, with great effort. Jamie was much like her. He had seen what love had done to his mother, robbed her of spirit. Could he prevent that from happening to Jamie? The very thing that he admired most about her would be the one thing looked down upon by his people. Did it truly matter that much what his people thought?

Grabbing his pajamas from nearby, Ben slipped them on and walked back into the bedroom. He would go to Jamie. Talk to her again. Keep vigil at her bedside since she would probably not allow him in her bed. He still must remember his duty to her. He must guard her with his life. Tomorrow they would discuss the rest.

The bedside lamp and bathroom light shut off simultaneously. Instinctively, Ben's gaze snapped to the security system panel attached to the wall near his bedroom door. No red light glowed to indicate that the alarm was functioning.

Ben raced from the bedroom at a run, his heart keeping time with his gait, only one goal on his mind.

Reaching Jamie before it was too late.

The floorboard squeaked beneath Jamie's feet, startling her. The hallway was dark, very dark, and she felt eerily disturbed. Usually Alima left the bathroom light on for her. But not tonight.

Knowing Alima, she was probably trying to create an atmosphere for lovers. If the woman only knew how successful Jamie had been in her seduction—how hopelessly in love she was with Ben—would Alima tell her I told you so? Could be, and Jamie deserved her scorn and much more.

Feeling along the wall, Jamie found the doorknob to her room, turned it and pushed the door open.

A hand grabbed her arm and yanked her inside.

A moist palm clamped over her mouth, inhibiting her respiration.

Blind panic contracted her chest when she was pulled back against the unknown assailant. The stench of cigarettes and sweat seeped into her nostrils, causing her stomach to roil. But the feel of something cold and hard jabbed in her side made her want to collapse from fear.

"Miss Morris, so we finally meet again."

Jamie tried to scream but all she could manage was a moan. She tried to struggle, which only caused the man's grip to tighten on her mouth.

"Don't move, or I will be forced to harm you."

Jamie froze, her ears ringing, her heart pounding.

His evil chuckle made her quake. "I must say, Payune did not know what he was missing by ending your marriage agreement. He would be pleasantly surprised to know that one so young is such an expert lover." His demented voice was laced with a heavy European accent. A voice that seemed somewhat familiar to Jamie, but she couldn't remember where she'd heard it.

His whiskey-laden breath fanned the side of her face and she tightly closed her eyes. "I see that the sheikh has fallen for your charms. I am surprised he sent you to your room alone when he could so obviously have had you again. But I am grateful for that fact, since you have something I need."

Jamie bit back the nausea and wished with all her might she could bite him. Not possible with his hand held so tightly against her mouth.

"I want that wedding dress," he demanded, venom in his tone.

Why did he want her mother's dress? Did it have to do with that mysterious *something?* Obviously, but she had no clue what.

"I will uncover your mouth," he said, "but should you make the slightest sound other than telling me the where-abouts of the dress, I will kill you." He forced the gun farther into her ribcage, leaving Jamie no doubt he was serious.

Where was Ben? In his room, she decided, stewing over her refusal to marry him. She'd been such a fool, and her foolishness could very well cost her her life. Maybe even Ben's life. She prayed he stayed in his room, away from danger. Then she could die knowing he was safe.

What was she thinking? She wasn't going to die, at least not without a fight. She needed an opportunity, just a small window of time, and then she could act.

"Do you promise not to scream?" he asked. She nodded her agreement. "Good."

He slowly lowered his hand and turned her to face him. She coughed, gagged, then drew in several ragged breaths. Staring at his shadowy frame, she couldn't make out his features, but she could tell he wasn't very big. Maybe an inch or two taller than she. A point in her favor should she decide to make a move.

He fingered a lock of her hair and laughed, sending icy chills of apprehension up her spine like fingers on piano keys. "I am sorry we have no lights so I can see you better, but I'm afraid that is my fault. Although when I watched you and your lover in action, I did see quite well. I truly enjoyed your, what shall I call it? Display of affection?" He touched her face and she cringed. "Had I more time, I might partake of your talents. But I am in a hurry, so perhaps later then?''

''Over my dead body,'' Jamie hissed.

He jabbed the gun into her belly, causing her to wince. ''That could be arranged, but first the dress. Where is it!''

''In the closet, over there.'' She pointed a shaky finger toward the double doors across the room. When the creep turned his head in that direction, Jamie took her chance. She thrust her knee up into his groin with all her might, hitting the bull's-eye.

Startled, he dropped the gun to grab his crotch. Jamie immediately turned and ran into the solid wall of a chest. This time she did scream.

''I am here, Jamie.''

Ben. Thank God.

Pushing her aside, Ben took the man to the ground in one heavy thud. Jamie's eyes had adjusted to the limited light, allowing her to look on in terror as Ben struggled with the assailant. Two dark figures rolling on the floor. Where was the gun?

A light flickered behind Jamie, casting frightening shadows on the wall. She turned toward the glow to find Alima standing in the doorway, holding a large candle.

''What is this?'' Alima asked, horror in her voice.

''This is Robert Klimt,'' Ben growled. ''Murderer. Thief.''

When Jamie realized Ben had the intruder pinned to the ground, she let out a breath of relief and moved toward the pair, Alima following close behind. After she grabbed a robe from the chair and slipped it on, she kicked something with her toe and looked down. The gun. Slowly she picked it up and held it trained on Klimt's leg, the only place not covered by Ben who now straddled him with his hands

wrapped around Klimt's throat. The man's eyes bulged
with panic. Jamie wanted to cheer.

"Bring the candle closer," Jamie told Alima.

Alima slowly moved forward and in the candle's glow,
Jamie studied Klimt's small sharp features, the mole near
his left brow, and remembered.

"He was on the plane," Jamie said.

"Yes. He was trying to escape to freedom." Ben jerked
Klimt's head up. "Where did you hide the diamond?" The
fear didn't lessen in Klimt's face, yet he didn't speak.

"Diamond?" Jamie asked. "What diamond?"

"The diamond this animal stole after he killed the club's
bartender, Riley Monroe." Ben lowered his voice to a menacing tone. "Is that correct, Robert Klimt? You killed a
defenseless man after you forced him to take you to the
jewels?"

"I admit nothing."

Ben let Klimt's head hit the floor with a *thunk,* but kept
his grip around the man's neck. "You will admit everything."

The man tried to wrench Ben's hands away but couldn't.
He made a choking sound. "Again, I ask. Where is the
diamond?" Ben commanded.

Jamie worried that Ben might kill Klimt before he had
his answer if she didn't do something to stop him. "I think
it has something to do with my mother's dress," she said
quickly. "Or he thinks it does. He demanded I give it to
him."

Ben loosened his hold on Klimt's neck. "Is that where
we will find the diamond?"

Klimt looked a bit too cocky for someone with hands
wrapped around his windpipe. "And what will happen to
me if I tell you?"

Ben sneered. "It is what I will do to you if you do not tell me that should concern you."

"I will be no good to you dead."

"He's right, Ben," Jamie said, grasping for anything to help Ben regain some common sense.

Ben looked at her for a moment before again turning his attention to Klimt. "If I should decide to spare your life, you will be turned over to the Asterland authorities. They will deal with you as they see fit. Or perhaps I will release you to the Americans and let them handle this. First-degree murder in the state of Texas carries with it death by execution." Ben's ensuing smile was cynical. "Perhaps that would be best."

Klimt's eyes bulged with terror. "No. You cannot do that. I have diplomatic immunity. I am a respected man in my country. I am a—"

"—*tays bawáal,*" Alima shouted, cutting off Klimt's protests. When Jamie stared at her, Alima added, "A pissing he-goat."

An adequate description, Jamie decided.

"Give me the bedsheet," Ben said.

Alima hurried to the bed, stripped off the sheet, and offered it to Ben. With one hand still clasped around Klimt's throat, he took the sheet then grasped Klimt's wrists and dragged him across the floor to the bed. He raised the man's hands and tied them to the bedpost, leaving him helplessly suspended with his arms over his head like a side of beef.

Ben turned to Jamie. "Give me the gun."

She'd forgotten she was still holding it. With shaking hands, she complied.

Stepping back, Ben pointed the pistol at Klimt's head. "Now, tell me everything."

"If I do cooperate, will you assure me that you will

speak to the Asterland authorities and tell them I have aided you in the investigation?''

''Is that in hope they will give you a lighter sentence?'' Ben's laugh was sharp, without humor. ''I would rather deal with you myself than risk that you will not be adequately punished for the crimes you have committed. For killing my friend.''

''I will not speak again unless I have your promise.''

Ben rubbed a hand over his shadowed jaw, indecision warring in his expression. ''I will see what I can do, but I make no promises where your country is concerned.''

Klimt lowered his head in defeat. ''I did kill your Riley Monroe because it was necessary. After he led me to the jewels, I could not risk him revealing my identity. I planned to sell the jewels to fund the revolution.''

''Is Payune connected to this scheme?''

''I act alone for the sake of the revolution.''

Jamie shivered to think her once-intended was somehow involved in all this mess, even though Klimt denied it.

''We recovered all the jewels but the red diamond,'' Ben said. ''Where is it now?''

''You will find the diamond sewn into the hem of the wedding dress.''

Ben's jaw tensed, and Jamie sensed he was barely hanging on to his restraint. ''You are lying. Miss Morris has told me the dress was not out of her possession.''

Klimt glared at her with hate-filled eyes. ''She is mistaken. The dress was taken to the cleaners two days before we were to depart for Asterland. I broke into the shop and put the diamond there myself before she retrieved it.''

Jamie's mouth gaped when she realized the man was telling the truth. How stupid of her not to remember. ''I'm sorry, Ben, I didn't even think about that. I was only thinking about after the plane crash.''

"It is all right, Jamie," Ben said in a gentle voice. "It no longer matters." He pulled her to his side, taking her by surprise. "Did this swine harm you, Jamie? If so, I will kill him now."

"No!" Jamie couldn't let Ben kill Klimt no matter what the vile man had done. Ben would then risk going to jail himself. "He didn't do anything except try to scare me to death."

"Then I will let him live. For now." He turned to Alima. "Go and find J.D. He should be on the porch, although I have my doubts since he allowed Klimt access to the house."

"Your man is on the porch, asleep," Klimt said.

"I'm right here, you sorry S.O.B."

Everyone looked toward the door where J.D. now stood holding a flashlight, a small trickle of blood streaming from his forehead. He pointed at Klimt. "This coward ambushed me, knocked me over the head with some kind of pipe. Then he stole my danged gun."

Ben walked to J.D. and handed him the weapon. "Stay here and make sure he does not move."

"You got it, boss." J.D. grabbed the gun and stood over Klimt, his lips curled up into a menacing snarl.

Ben took Jamie by the shoulders and turned her to face him, away from Klimt. "You are safe now."

Jamie could only nod when she saw the concern in his expression.

Ben walked to the closet and removed the wedding dress. He laid it across the bed carefully. Jamie and Alima gathered round as he examined the hem. With a fingertip, he tore away several threads and reached inside. "It is here."

Alima lowered the candle and centered it on Ben's large palm holding a round red jewel sparkling in the flickering light. Jamie had never seen anything quite like it, at least five carats, she assumed. Red in color, it resembled a ruby.

"Who does it belong to?" Jamie asked.

Ben closed his hand over it. "To the town of Royal, its rightful owners."

"I've heard the legend of the jewels," Jamie said, "but I never believed they really existed."

"Yes, they do. And you must promise you'll never tell anyone of their existence. To do so will again bring about more fortune hunters such as this one." He nodded toward Klimt.

Jamie vowed to carry the secret to her grave. "I promise."

"Go with Alima now," he told her. "I will return to you as soon as I make arrangements to have Klimt removed." He brushed a kiss across her forehead before turning to J.D. "If he should lift a finger, you have my permission to shoot him."

J.D. laughed. "That'll be my pleasure, boss."

Ben took the flashlight from J.D. then headed out the door.

Jamie glared at the man who'd almost killed her twice now, and had the strongest urge to kick him again. But he looked so small and pitiful. Harmless, actually. Still, she would like to vent her frustration somehow. Maybe she should just tickle him under the arms. Death by uncontrollable laughter.

Alima's hand on her arm prevented her from giving in to the impulse, which was just as well. J.D. might actually shoot him if she made the creep move, and she didn't want his death on her conscience no matter what he'd put her through.

"Come, child," Alima said. "We will go to the kitchen. I will prepare you a drink to help you sleep, and you can tell me why this man is hanging from your bed."

Eight

Ben stood at his front doorway watching until the taillights disappeared from sight. Justin Webb and Matthew Walker had just left with the red diamond—the last of the three stolen jewels—and Robert Klimt. They intended to lock both of them up—Klimt in the Cattleman's Club basement until they arranged for him to return to Asterland, and the jewel with the other two until they could find another hiding place. Now it was of the utmost importance that they make plans to thwart the impending revolution. But that would come later in the day. At the moment, Ben needed to see about Jamie.

After searching the kitchen and living room, he found her curled up on the small sofa in his bedroom, covered by a silk throw, her eyes closed. Dawn's light seeped through the curtained window, washing her beautiful face in an ethereal glow. She appeared angelic, at peace. For that Ben was glad.

Deciding not to disturb her, he turned away.

"Ben?"

Her magnetic voice pulled him around to face her again. "I did not mean to wake you."

"I wasn't asleep. I'm too afraid to sleep."

He moved to the sofa and pulled her into his arms. She trembled against him. "It is all right now, Jamie. He is gone. He cannot hurt you anymore. You are safe with me."

The warmth of her lips against his neck brought his exhausted body to life. Tipping her chin up, he kissed her face, tasted the salt of her tears. She had been so courageous, so strong, but now she wilted like yesterday's flowers. And he needed her desperately.

Slipping his arms beneath her, he picked her up and took her to his bed, following her down onto the satin sheets. She clung to him and sobbed. He held her, stroked her hair, brushed a kiss over her lips and whispered words of consolation. He knew not what else to do. He wanted to make love to her, but he was afraid. Afraid she would turn him away.

She didn't. Instead, she drew his head down and kissed him in earnest, clutching at the T-shirt he wore. Filled with impatient need, he sat up and tore the shirt over his head, then shed his jeans while she slipped her gown off and tossed it aside. He came back to her and ran greedy hands over her naked flushed body, taking each curve to memory. She arched against him when he drew her nipple into his mouth and suckled. She moaned when he slipped his fingertips through the cleft between her thighs. He found her wet and warm, ready for him. Yet he took his time, stroking her slowly to build the tension higher, until he knew she could hold out no longer.

When her breaths became sharp gasps, he joined with her, sinking into her tight sheath. She wrapped her legs about him, drawing him farther into her welcoming heat, and sending her farther into his soul. He wanted to temper his movements, savor the moment, but he could no longer ignore his own body's demand when she writhed beneath him.

Clinging to his last shred of control, he stopped moving and slipped from her body, determined not to succumb to his release until she had been fulfilled. Jamie gave a little moan of protest, urging a smile from Ben.

He sat up and grasped her waist. "This way will be better for you," he said.

It didn't take long for understanding to dawn in her expression when Ben lay back. She moved over him, straddling his body. Slowly, she lowered herself onto his shaft, her face melting into pure pleasure.

Ben steeled against the heady sensations and willed himself to hang on for a little longer. "You are in control, Jamie," he whispered. "Do with me what you will."

If he could give her no more, he could give her this.

Ben kept his gaze locked into hers. She was now in complete command of her body and his. He watched her expression change like a chameleon as she found independence in their lovers' dance. Her face went slack and her eyes drifted shut. Her bottom lip trembled and a long steady moan left her lips. Only then did Ben give in to his own release and let go as never before.

Jamie collapsed against him, her heart drumming at his chest to match the rhythm of his own heart. He held her tightly in fear she might slip away, as if she were a dream of his own making. But she was not a dream. She was real. So very real.

He had never experienced such satisfaction. Such a sense of total completeness. She had crept under his skin, stolen his heart and soul. And as sleep overtook him, he vowed he would never let her go.

"Where are you going?"

Jamie's hand paused on the open drawer before she picked up the last of her underclothes and stuffed them in the bag she'd brought with her. "I'm going home."

"No, you are not."

Her gaze snapped to his. Ben stood in the doorway dressed in his Arabian clothes, appearing commanding and in control, and oh so gorgeous. She looked away again, worried she'd give in to him if she didn't. "You can't stop me. Klimt's out of the picture, so that means I can return to my apartment, find a job. Get on with my life."

She sensed his presence behind her. "Then you will not consider my proposal?"

"I can't, Ben." She turned to face him, shocked by the hurt in his gray eyes. "I have to sort things out. Figure out what I'm going to do next. Be my own person."

"I will allow you to do these things."

"Allow me?" She grabbed the bag and carried it to the bed. "You see, Ben, that's the problem. I don't want anyone *allowing* me anything like I'm some teenager who doesn't know her own mind. I want to go back to school. I want to be an adult and take care of myself."

"Then you are saying you do not want me?"

Oh, she wanted him all right. She wanted him like nothing she'd ever wanted before. But she couldn't have him. Not when he saw her as nothing more than an obligation. "What we've shared has been great. You've taught me a lot of things, including the fact that I can make it on my own."

"Even after what we have experienced together, you would still leave me?" he asked, frustration in his voice.

"Would you give yourself so freely without anything in return?"

He had no idea what he'd given her, and she would never forget it. Forget him. "I have no choice."

"Yes, you do. Marry me."

"I can't."

His gaze slid away for a moment before returning to her, defeat in his eyes. "Is there nothing I can say to convince you?"

Yes, there was something he could say, but she knew in her heart he wouldn't. She swallowed around the boulder in her throat. "I'll never forget what we've shared. But I have to move on. So do you. You need to find a woman who can give you lots of babies and quietly tend to your needs. I'm not that woman."

"Yet you may be carrying my child."

"I'll deal with that if it has happened."

He came to her in a rush and grasped her arms. "If it is so, you must tell me. The child will be mine."

So now she understood all too well. Ben viewed everything as a possession. No way was she falling into that trap. "Like I said, I'll deal with it."

"I will not leave you alone."

"If you don't, I'll leave town."

"I will find you."

"Maybe, maybe not," she said, although she knew he had the money and means to find her, no matter where she might go. But she couldn't worry about that now. She hoped he would simply respect her wishes and stay out of her life. "Now would you please unhand me so I can go home?"

His dark eyes narrowed, and he pulled her to him. His lips met hers in a hard bruising kiss. A kiss full of frustration, of passion. Then he released her and stepped back.

"I will let you leave now, but remember, I do not easily give up. You may trust me on that."

Ben tried to concentrate on the conversation between his fellow Cattleman's Club members but again found it increasingly difficult, as it had been the last time they'd met. His thoughts kept turning to Jamie, the way she had driven away in her battered blue car that morning, out of his life, but never out of his mind.

"So he didn't say for sure whether or not Payune was connected?"

Ben looked up to find Aaron Black addressing him. "He claims he acted alone. But I do not believe him."

"Neither do we," Black said. "That's why we've decided Dakota will go to Asterland and try to straighten this mess out."

"Where is the diamond?" Ben asked.

Aaron Black hooked a thumb over his shoulder. "With the others behind the plaque."

"And Klimt?"

"On a plane back to his country," Justin said. "They promised to deal with him appropriately."

Ben released a harsh laugh. "I doubt they will do to him what he deserves after what he has done to Jamie."

The members exchanged knowing glances before Black spoke again. "I've been in touch with Kathy Lewis, and she's agreed to make the trip with Dakota."

Dakota Lewis's frame went rigid. "So she did agree."

"Yeah, and she's on her way here," Justin said.

Ben studied Dakota's expression, his anger evident in the way he gripped the arms of his chair. "I don't know why you all think that involving my ex-wife in this mess is going to help."

"She has connections to Asterland's queen," Matt said. "We need her."

Dakota tossed aside a pen and watched it roll to the floor. "Is there no other way?"

"Nope," Justin said. "It's the perfect cover. Husband and wife traveling to Asterland on the pretense it's a second honeymoon."

"It will never work," Lewis said, his tone laced with frustration. "I'm not that good an actor."

"Look, Dakota," Black said. "I know you and Kathy have a history, but you're just going to have to bite the bullet and think about what we'd be losing if the current Asterland government falls. We all have strong business connections there, and we owe it not only to the king, but to ourselves to try and prevent that from happening."

"It is the only way," Ben stated, knowing in fact that his investments would suffer if they did not succeed with this plan. And he would like nothing better than to have Payune punished for his involvement. After all, the man was responsible for putting Jamie in danger, whether Klimt admitted it or not.

"Then it's settled?" Justin asked.

Dakota looked away. "Yeah, it's settled."

Aaron Black stood. "Great. We'll be in touch. Right now I've got to get back to Pamela. She wants to go shopping for baby stuff."

Everyone laughed then, except Ben. He again considered that Jamie might be carrying his child. Would she tell him, or would she possibly leave town without him knowing for certain? He could not allow that. And if she did try to run, he would find her, as he had promised. He would use every option available to him. Perhaps she would come to him on her own. Perhaps he was insane for believing that might be possible.

Justin, Dakota and Aaron took their leave, but Matt remained seated across from Ben, surveying him suspiciously.

Matt leaned forward and folded his hands before him. "So, where's Jamie?"

"She has returned to her apartment."

"Oh, yeah? I thought maybe you two might have hit it off. I was thinking maybe you'd tell us we have another wedding to look forward to."

"She refused my proposal." Ben wanted to take back the admission the moment it left his idiotic mouth.

"Then there *was* more to it than Big Ben playing the bodyguard."

Ben shifted in his chair. "Yes, but I did not intend for it to happen."

"Neither did I, Ben, my boy. But it did. So what do you plan to do now?"

"I do not know."

"You're not going to just let her get away, are you?"

Ben drummed the table with his fingers, impatience closing in on him. "I fear she is already gone."

Matt laughed. "Ben, you beat all. I've never seen you give up on anything so easily. Unless what happened doesn't mean that much to you?"

Ben's gaze snapped to Matt's, anger seeping from every pore. "I do not view her in that light. I have come to understand her. To respect her. I have come to…" He let the words trail away, afraid to claim them. Afraid to voice them. To make them real.

"You're in love with her, aren't you?"

Ben tried to close off Matt's question, but to no avail. "I am not certain. I have never experienced love for a woman."

Matt grinned. "Do you feel like you've lost your best

friend at the same time you just came close to sealing a million-dollar deal and the contract fell through?''

"Yes."

"Then face it, Ben. You're in love with her. Lock, stock and barrel. But any one of us could tell that the minute you walked through the door a few days ago."

"It does not matter now. She will not see me."

"Then you'll just have to try harder. Woo her."

Ben frowned. "Woo her?"

"Yeah, you know. Do things for her. Make her realize she can't live without you." Matt slapped a palm on the table. "And I'll send Helena over to talk to her. We have the same situation in reverse. You and Helena are from royal blood, different worlds. Jamie and I are just plain folk. But Helena and I have worked out our differences. She could probably help."

A small weight lifted from Ben's heart. "Do you think that would be possible?"

"It's a start. But you've got to participate, too."

"I have no idea where to begin."

Matt released a frustrated sigh. "Ben, use that head of yours for something other than your investments. Buy her nice things. Cook her dinner. Be creative."

The purchasing of gifts was something Ben could manage without any trouble, but he had never even lifted a pot from the stove, much less prepared a meal. He supposed Alima could teach him something to make for Jamie. Perhaps hot dogs.

Ben rose, ready to put his plan in action. "I will consider your suggestions."

Matt stood. "I'll send Helena to Jamie's soon. She'll be glad to get out of the house now that Klimt's been caught."

Ben offered his hand for a shake. "Wish me luck, *Sadíiq*. I will need it."

"I have no doubt you'll do fine," Matt said, grinning.

Unfortunately, Ben had grave doubts. But he vowed they would not stop him. He would not give up until he had Jamie Morris back in his bed, in his life, for good.

Jamie collapsed onto the sofa, relieved she had her old job at the hospital back. Her life back. Without Ben.

The man was truly amazing. She'd come home to her apartment expecting to dive into much-needed clean-up due to the break-in. Instead, she'd found everything back in its place, along with all new furniture, compliments of Sheikh Ben Rassad. Obviously he was trying to buy his way back into her life. Jamie refused to give in to those tactics.

But no matter how hard she tried to forget him, he'd preyed on her mind night and day for the past week. She didn't miss being cooped up in his house, but she did miss him. Terribly. She missed Alima, too. Although the housekeeper had never asked about Jamie's and Ben's relationship, Jamie suspected she knew what had transpired between them. Yet she'd never said I told you so. She had simply told Jamie to take care and not to give up on matters of the heart.

Jamie had all but given up. She had no desire to look for a replacement for Ben. No one would ever measure up.

The knock at the door startled Jamie. Glancing at the clock, she wondered who would be calling on her at 8:00 p.m.

Ben?

She was thrilled by that prospect, yet afraid to find him on her doorstep. What would she say to him?

When the bell rang, Jamie rose and moved to the door, steeling herself in case she should find a sheikh on the other side. She peered through the peephole, but it wasn't Ben at all. Lady Helena Reichard stood in the hallway, impeccably dressed, blond hair pulled into a neat chignon, her pastel-blue silk suit looking as though she, too, had been on a job interview.

Throwing open the door, Jamie grinned. "Helena? I can't believe you're here!"

Helena held up a large white box. "Yes, I'm here, and I brought some of Manny's apple pie. Can I come in?"

Jamie stepped aside. "Of course."

Helena moved past her, favoring her left leg, and set the box on the table before facing Jamie again. "Your apartment looks wonderful. You've been busy redecorating, I take it."

Jamie looked around as if seeing it for the first time. "Actually, I didn't do it. Ben…Sheikh Rassad is responsible for the changes." He was responsible for many changes, but Jamie wouldn't burden Helena with her problems, not considering everything the woman had been through since the whole Asterland mess had started. Helena had been burned in the crash, her ankle shattered, yet she had managed to come through like a trooper. Now she had a new fiancé in rancher Matt Walker, a wedding planned in the next few months, and a new life in America.

Jamie tried to tamp down the envy as she pulled back a chair at the sparkling new dinette. Helena deserved Jamie's admiration and respect, not jealousy over her good fortune. "Have a seat and tell me what brings you here."

Helena settled in and Jamie noticed the mesh glove hiding the burns on Helena's left hand. She felt an immediate pang of sympathy—and guilt over not going to see Helena the minute she'd left Ben's ranch.

"I thought we were due a visit," Helena said. "Now that things seem to be safer in Royal, thanks to your Ben, I decided we needed to talk."

"He's not *my* Ben," Jamie said adamantly, then regretted the harsh words. "I mean, he's just a friend. Was a friend. He was very good to me while I was staying at his place."

Helena raised a thinly arched brow. "Really? He's a very attractive man. Maybe you discovered a little romance?"

"Actually, I—" Jamie saw no sense in hiding it from Helena. Since the crash, the woman had been the closest thing to a good friend that Jamie had known. Except maybe Alima. And Ben. "Yeah, I guess you could say that. We became rather...close."

Helena sent her a kind, knowing smile. "So I've heard from Matt."

Jamie frowned. "Was Ben bragging about it? If he was, then I'm going to march right out there to the ranch and—"

Helena laid a hand on Jamie's arm. "No, he wasn't boasting. Matt told me that Ben's moping around most of the time—lovesick."

If only Jamie could believe that. "Take my word for it, he's not in love with me. In lust with me, maybe, but not in love."

"Are you certain?"

"Yes. He never told me he loved me. He did ask me to marry him after... Well, after we became close."

"After you made love?" Helena added without judgment.

Jamie needed to explain. She valued Helena's respect, and she didn't want the woman thinking badly of her. "I didn't exactly mean for anything to happen between us, it just did." She lowered her eyes, away from Helena's steady perusal. "Truth is, I seduced him, not the other way around. I couldn't help myself. I'd never been with a man before, and he was just so...so..."

"Irresistible?" Helena laughed. "I know exactly what you mean. I feel the same about Matthew. They're both enigmatic men, strong, passionate. Not easy attributes for a woman to resist.''

"You can say that again,'' Jamie said wistfully. "I've never met anyone quite like Ben.''

"Nor have I met anyone like Matt. And I love him with all my heart.'' Helena leaned forward, her blue eyes intent and serious. "Do you love Ben, Jamie?''

Jamie wanted to burst into tears, but she held back by sheer will. "I don't know, I guess.'' Why was she lying? "Yes, I love him. More than I ever imagined loving anyone. He's so stubborn and demanding at times. So different from me because of his culture. He's used to women being passive. I'm anything but that. I don't want to be that at all. I'm afraid if I accept Ben's marriage proposal, he won't be happy with the real me, and I can't change who I am.''

"Marriage proposal?'' Helena placed a hand on her chest. "Matt didn't tell me Ben proposed to you.''

"Yes, he did, because he felt obligated to marry me since he 'took my virginity.' Have you ever heard of anything so backward in your life?''

"I find it honorable that he would care enough to ask you to marry him.''

"I don't want him to marry me because he feels obligated.''

"Maybe you should give Ben another chance to prove himself to you, considering how you feel about him.''

Jamie centered her gaze on Helena. "He's already proved his honor by protecting me. Now I want only one thing from him. I want him to say he loves me. Is that too much to ask?''

"From a man like Ben? Possibly. Words might not come easily for him. In fact, I'm not certain he realizes he is in love with you. But I gather he is rather pitiful right now and it's only a matter of time before he does make that realization. And look at it this way. He could have any woman he wants, but it seems he has chosen you."

Jamie stood and walked into the adjacent kitchen to make some tea. "I don't know if that's enough."

Helena joined her at the counter. "What I'm about to tell you is between you and me. I wanted to come see you, but I planned to do it two days from now when I came into town for my doctor's appointment. Matt convinced me to come earlier after he met with Ben. He told me the sheikh's a wreck, so he offered to have me come and speak with you."

Hurt niggled at Jamie's heart. "So this was a set-up orchestrated by Ben and Matt?"

"No, Jamie. I agreed to do it not because Ben or Matt wanted it, but because I want you to understand that no matter what differences two people might have from a cultural standpoint, love has an amazing way of spanning those boundaries."

Jamie tried not to hope. "Do you really think so?"

Helena put her arm around Jamie's shoulder and gave her a gentle squeeze. "All I'm saying is keep an open mind. Give it some time. Time really does heal all wounds." She held up her injured hand. "I'm counting on that. So have faith in your heart, and give Ben a second chance."

Should she really follow Helena's advice? Could she really open her heart that wide? "I'll think about it, but I haven't even heard from him. He's probably changed his mind."

"You never know," Helena said with a smile. "And if I were you, I'd be prepared for anything."

Jamie wasn't at all prepared the next morning when two floral delivery trucks pulled up at the curb while she was attempting to head to the hospital for work. The deliverymen opened their sliding van doors and carried in vases full of every flower imaginable, two at a time, while Jamie stood by speechless. By the time they were done, Jamie's entire apartment was covered in blooms, from roses to carnations to daisies and some beautiful orange blossoms that Jamie had never seen before.

They were all from Ben, or so the card on the largest vase full of pink roses declared. The message read, Marry me—Ben. Not Love, With love, I love you, or any endearment whatsoever. Jamie tried not to be too disappointed, but she couldn't help it. Ben was trying to buy his way back into her life.

Not a chance she would give in that quickly.

Once she reached the hospital, she picked up the phone and dialed his number. Fortunately, Alima answered.

"Is Ben in?" she asked the housekeeper.

"Jamie, child, is that you?"

"Yes, it's me. I need to talk with your boss."

"I am afraid he is not present. He has left today for Canada, and I do not expect him until tomorrow morning."

That was probably best, Jamie decided. If she heard his deep magnetic voice, no telling what she might say or do. "Just leave him a message, please. Tell him I loved the flowers, but I'm not a blooming idiot."

A long silence filled the line. "I do not write English well."

"Then tell him thanks, but no thanks."

"He will be most disappointed he could not speak with you. Should I have him call you?"

"No!" Jamie lowered her voice when she saw another transcriptionist peek from behind a nearby cubicle. "Just tell him what I said."

"As you wish, Jamie. I would like to say that I greatly miss your company. I have no one with whom to view my television programs."

"Maybe we can do that again some day." A promise Jamie shouldn't make. She had no intention of returning to the ranch. "You could come here to my place. I'm off on Thursdays. We could just hang around and watch the soaps all day. Veg out on the couch."

"I do not understand this 'veg out.' Do you mean cook the vegetables?"

"No, act like one." Jamie could picture Alima shaking her head. "Well, I need to go. And I miss you, too."

"I am glad," Alima said, a smile in her voice. "The sheikh misses you terribly. I believe he suffers from a broken heart."

Jamie's own heart dropped over the declaration. "I'm sure he'll recover quickly once he goes home again." Home to his mistresses with no commitment, no ties.

"He will not leave, although his mother has called several times since your departure. He claims he still has unfinished business."

"I hope he finishes it soon," Jamie said. "I'm sure his mother misses him, too." As much as Jamie missed him.

"I would assume that, but I believe his unfinished business involves you."

"There's nothing unfinished between us, Alima. It's over."

"Nothing is over until the large woman sings."

Jamie stifled a laugh. Alima had finally adopted some American sayings, even though they weren't quite accurate. "I suppose, but don't count on it."

"I only count on two things, dear Jamie. The sun rising in the east, and the power of love between a man and a woman. You would do well to remember that."

Alima said a brief goodbye and hung up, leaving Jamie to ponder her words. Yes, there was a lot of power in love, but Ben didn't really love her. He wanted to own her, and Jamie refused to be owned by any man. Even a man she loved.

Nine

"**D**oes Miss Morris know you're comin' here tonight?"

Ben smiled at the elderly landlord and prepared to lie. "Yes, she knows. I am making her dinner." He nodded toward the paper sacks in his arms.

The man eyed him with suspicion, angering Ben. He had advanced the landlord six months' rent on Jamie's apartment after Klimt ravaged the place. He had spoken to him several times by phone to ascertain that Jamie's apartment was still safe. He had arranged for him to let the delivery-man in to set up the new furniture. Surely by those gestures alone the proprietor realized that Ben's intentions were honorable where Jamie was concerned.

"Mr. Grable, I assure you that Miss Morris would not mind you opening the door for me."

A long moment of silence passed before the landlord spoke again. "Well, I s'pose it would be okay for me to let you in seeing as how you did help her out with her rent and all."

"Thank you for your consideration."

With agonizing slowness, the man slipped a key in the lock and pushed open the door. He turned back to Ben, still looking reluctant. "I sure hope she don't get mad at me. You be sure to tell her this was all your idea."

"I will be certain to inform Miss Morris of your kindness."

The man left Ben standing on the threshold of Jamie's apartment without further protest. Ben stepped inside, pleased to find that the flowers he'd sent were still intact, not torn to shreds. When he'd arrived home that morning, Alima had given him Jamie's message. That would not stop him from his mission. Tonight was only the beginning of his "wooing."

Making his way into the small kitchen, he set the bags on the small counter and surveyed his surroundings, feeling as foreign as he had when he'd first come to America.

How difficult could it be to prepare this simple meal? Economics had been his college major, and he'd mastered all the upper-level courses with ease. He had handled many of his own investments and had proven successful in all his financial endeavors. He could most certainly make hot dogs.

Ben rifled through the bag and withdrew the frankfurters, a can of Texas chili, a package of buns, and a small plastic bottle of mustard. The other bag held two bottles of champagne he'd had the Cattleman's Club's new bartender order. The best that money could buy, fitting for a grand celebration. Ben hoped that by the time this plan was complete, both he and Jamie would have something to celebrate.

Ben read the directions on the package of franks. They

were vague at best. With little time before Jamie returned home from her job, he opted to use the microwave, although he had never operated one before. Surely this would also be an elementary task. Opening a cabinet, he took out two gold-rimmed dishes. Fine china. He was pleasantly surprised that Jamie would own such nice things after claiming she had simple tastes.

Standing in front of the microwave, Ben stared at the buttons in hopes they would soon make sense. The directions on the hot dogs stated to heat each one for 30 seconds. Since he was warming three, Ben set the timer for five minutes to assure they were completely done. He had never cared for the fare, and he certainly did not enjoy the thought of eating cold wieners.

He wrestled with the electric can-opener for a time. The can of chili slipped from the magnet, landing on the counter with a thud. He poured the contents into a pan and set it on the stove with the temperature turned to High. Feeling proud that he had managed thus far, Ben smiled with satisfaction as he tore open the package of buns. Simple. Why had he believed this would be so difficult?

A loud pop startled Ben, and his gaze shot to the microwave that seemed to be shooting sparks. Opening the door, he found the plate shattered, and the inside of the tomb covered in pink fleshy remains. What had he done wrong?

No matter. He would simply follow the directions to boil the wieners. At least he had plenty left.

A foul smell, followed by a gurgling noise, drew his attention. The chili erupted from the pan like a volcano, splattering the white countertops and floor with brown-orange blobs. Ben immediately grabbed for the pan without thinking. The handle seared his hand and he dropped the offending pot back onto the stove, sending the chili down the front of his neatly starched white shirt.

Now he was a mess. The kitchen was a mess. And much to his dismay, Jamie was standing at the door, glaring at him.

"What are you doing?" Her voice was low and surprisingly controlled.

"I am preparing dinner." Ben grabbed for a nearby dish towel and began rubbing at the spots on his shirt, avoiding her steely glare.

"It looks like you've had a food fight."

Yes, he had definitely been fighting with the food, and he was losing the battle. But he vowed not to give up. "I will clean the mess."

Jamie walked to the stove, grabbed a spoon from a white vase holding several utensils and began stirring the chili. "It's just a tad burned, Ben. I don't think it's edible in this state."

"Do you wish your hot dogs without the chili? Or I can return to the market and buy another can."

Jamie shook her head. "No. I'm not hungry."

Ben was. Hungry for the taste of her, the feel of her. She was dressed in snug black slacks and a red silk blouse. The pants adhered to her small bottom, defining her curves.

She turned to him and leaned back against the counter as if she had sensed his gaze. "What's this all about?"

Ben streaked a hand through his hair. "I wanted to surprise you. Prove to you that I would make a good husband."

She searched the kitchen war zone before returning her gaze to him. "I don't think you have a calling for the culinary arts."

"True, but if we are married, Alima would do the cooking for us."

She pinned him with her crystal-green eyes. "I like to cook, actually. And I really like living alone." Her gaze faltered, leading Ben to believe that like him, she had not enjoyed being alone at all.

Cautiously he moved toward her and brushed a long lock of golden hair from her shoulders. "I have missed you in my bed. I have missed your singing and your smile. Have you missed me?"

"I'm doing…just fine." She looked anywhere but directly at him.

"I believe you are lying."

She met his gaze, the familiar anger in her eyes. "I believe you've got an ego the size of Texas."

"Believe what you will," he said, bracing his hands on either side of the counter, "but I know that what we shared still haunts your dreams, as it does mine. I do not believe you can forget how well our bodies fit together, how much enjoyment we have taken from one another. How much remains to be shared between us."

With that, he took a chance and brought his lips to hers, leaning into her so that she would know how much he desired her. At first she tried to resist, but soon she opened to him and allowed him entry to the sweet recesses of her mouth. His whole being was consumed in fire generated by the kiss. The play of her tongue against his, the feel of her delicate body molded to his, drove him to near insanity. He wanted to take her right there, shove their clothing down and drive into her with the force of his need.

"No!" She pushed him back and ducked under his arm. He turned to find her backed up to the opposing wall, arms crossed over her chest. "You're not going to do this again. I'm not going to let you."

His gaze lingered over her body then came back to her flushed face. "It seems you already have."

She paced the kitchen and stopped at the open microwave. "What have you done to my grandmother's china?"

She spun around to face him and pointed toward the door. "Get out."

"Why? Do you not wish to acknowledge what is between us? Would you continue to deny it?"

"What's between us is chemistry. I want more."

"I will give you everything."

"You can't."

He took a step forward. "Tell me what you need, and I will search to the ends of the earth to find it for you."

"If you are too dumb to realize what I need from you, then you might as well give up."

Ben truly did not know what she needed from him that he had not already offered. How could he make her understand that he would do anything for her? How could he convince her that his life meant nothing without her in it?

He struggled to find the words to express himself, but they caught in his throat.

She sighed. "Ben, I'm tired. Please leave now."

He saw no point in continuing to beg her. He had another plan to develop, one that most surely would impress her. "I will clean up, then I will go."

"No, I'll do it. Go home. Let Alima fix you something decent to eat."

He no longer had an appetite for anything but Jamie's presence. "You are certain you wish me to leave?"

"Yes, I'm sure."

The familiar ache again settled on his heart. He was failing miserably at being a worthy man in her eyes. Yet he could not stand the thought of leaving her for good.

"All right, I will go tonight. But I will return."

She stomped her foot. "Don't you get it? I don't want you here. I don't need you here. Would you stop being so damned stubborn?"

"I will not stop until I have convinced you that we belong together."

Her eyes grew hazy with unclaimed tears, turning them a deeper emerald. Right then the urge to hold her again lived strong in Ben. But he refrained from giving in. Perhaps he would leave her be for a few days. His absence might convince her that she did miss him.

He turned and headed toward the door. With one hand braced on the knob, he said, "Pleasant dreams, my Jamie. I will be having them about you."

Jamie spent the next few days in a mental fog. Ben didn't call. Neither did her father. Never had she felt so alone. So confused. At least she had her work at the hospital and a few new friends she'd made in recent days. She'd even stopped by the local pet store and bought two goldfish to keep her company. Not that they provided all that much companionship.

After working her shift, including a few hours' overtime, she came home exhausted one evening to find two boxes on her dinette table—one large, one small—and a note from her landlord stating he'd personally delivered them to make sure they arrived safely, as ordered by the "Arabian man."

Prince Ben strikes again. What was he up to now?

After making some hot chamomile tea, Jamie sat at the table and stared at the boxes for a while, the pocketknife her father had given her on her twelfth birthday clutched in one hand, the teacup in the other. After a few moments, her curiosity got the best of her. She set the cup aside and picked up the smaller package. Slitting it open with the knife, she found beneath the packing a gold box from the Royal Confection Shoppe. She loved that place and often stopped by the window to admire the display, but she couldn't afford to buy any of their expensive candies.

Opening the lid, she found an array of dark chocolates—
her favorite—and in the middle, surrounded by the candies,
a small blue velvet box.

Jamie held her breath as she opened the hinged lid. A
ring, a brilliant oval diamond, surrounded by emeralds,
twinkled in the glow of the overhead light fixture. She had
never seen anything so beautiful in her life. It had to be at
least two carats and no telling how expensive.

Slipping the ring on her finger, she found it to be a perfect fit. She wasn't the least bit surprised, knowing it had
come from Ben. He would know her ring size. How, she
couldn't say. But he would, as surely as he knew her weakness for rich chocolates, something she had never told him.

Jamie turned her attention back to the candy and found
a slip of paper wedged between the edge of the box and
the paper shells. She unfolded the note and read.

I chose the emeralds to match the color of your eyes,
yet this ring does not compare to your beauty. I hope
that you will accept it as a token of my feelings for
you—Ben.

Feelings? What feelings? Okay, so maybe he did have
feelings for her. Maybe he did care for her. So why couldn't
he just say it?

She glanced at the other box and wondered how on earth
he could top the ring. The side was stamped Fragile, leading Jamie to believe it was something that could break as
easily as her heart had over the past few days.

Standing over the box, she again took the knife and carefully opened it. The inside was full of green squiggly foam
packing. She dug through the curly worms in a rush, sending them flying like jumping beans all over the table and

floor. Just beneath were several tissue-wrapped items. She tore into one and again couldn't believe her eyes.

A porcelain angel, and below that, more angels. All in varying shapes and sizes, many exact replicas of those belonging to her grandmother—the ones Klimt had destroyed with his careless disregard.

With each one she opened, another tear escaped down Jamie's cheek. How did Ben know how much these meant to her? How could he so easily bend her heart to his will?

Slumping into the chair, she clasped one delicate figurine in her hand and cried. Cried because she was so touched by the gesture. Cried because so many emotions crowded in on her.

She wanted to damn his persistence. She wanted to curse him for making her love him more. She wanted to call him and tell him to get his cute princely butt over here so she could show him her gratitude in wicked ways that would leave them both breathless. But she wouldn't. Not until she'd had more time to think.

With a sigh, she picked up the stack of envelopes that had come in the mail. Most were bills that needed to be paid. A lot of junk mail and credit-card solicitations. Some kind of notice from the bank. She opened that first, praying she wasn't overdrawn. Inside she found a letter, and her blood pressure rose with each word she read.

After she was finished, she slapped the letter on the table, yanked off the ring, and cursed the sheikh.

Ben Rassad had more nerve than a skydiver, and she was darn sure going to tell him he had gone too far this time.

Jamie stood on Ben's doorstep muttering a litany of curses that would have caused her mother to go for the lye soap. If only her mother were here now, telling her what to do next.

But she wasn't here, and Jamie had to handle this alone.

She punched the bell and waited, impatiently tapping her foot on the wooden porch, clutching the envelope in her hand. Earlier she had longed to see him again. Thank him. Hold him.

That was before she'd found the notice in the mail from the bank stating an anonymous benefactor had paid off the note to the farm in its entirety.

Anonymous. Ha! Jamie knew exactly who had that kind of money, and she was about to confront him. *If* he was home and not off rescuing some other damsel in distress.

The door opened to Alima, a bright smile on her face. "Jamie, you have returned! I am so happy to see you."

Jamie let go of her anger long enough to give the housekeeper a quick hug, then stepped back when she remembered why she was here. "Where's the sheikh?"

"In his study," Alima said warily. "Shall I summon him for you?"

"No. I think I'll just surprise him." Exactly like he'd surprised her.

Without waiting for Alima's response, Jamie strode through the great room and down the hall to Ben's office. She didn't even bother to knock.

After throwing the door open, she found him sitting at his desk, a stack of papers before him. She slapped the envelope in front of him. "How dare you."

He met her gaze with his serious gray eyes. "So you have come to see me after all."

"I've come to tell you that I don't appreciate what you've done. You had no right buying my father's farm."

He kicked back in the chair and propped his boots on the edge of the desk. Jamie tried not to notice his worn jeans, or the way his T-shirt strained across his broad chest when he braced his hands behind his head, the spattering of whiskers framing his sinfully sensual mouth. "I did not buy it. I simply paid off the note. Through my connections, I discovered the bank was in the process of foreclosing. Had I not put up the money, someone else would have purchased the farm and you would have lost everything."

She already felt as though she had lost everything. First her mother, then her father. More importantly, she'd lost her heart to this man sitting before her, looking confident and cocksure and way too sexy to ignore.

Jamie's pulse pounded in her ears. "I could've handled it myself had I known."

"Do you have that kind of money?"

"No...I..." Damn him! "I would have found it somewhere."

He slipped his feet from the desk and sat forward. "I have done this for you, Jamie. For your father. Can you not see that I care what happens to you both?"

She crossed her arms and shifted her weight from one foot to the other. "You don't even know my father."

"No, I do not. But I do know where he is. I have spoken with him."

Jamie dropped her arms to her sides and fisted her hands. "Where is he? How did you find him? I've asked everyone I know, and not one soul knows where he is."

"As I have told you, I have the means to find anyone."

Worry suddenly replaced Jamie's anger. No matter what her father had done in the past, she was still concerned for his well-being. "Is he okay?"

"He is safe. He has been residing at a private treatment facility. A place in the southern part of Texas that aids those with alcoholism. He has been getting help for his problem."

Jamie wanted desperately to cry, but she held back the

threatening tears, kept her hurt in check. "Why hasn't he been in touch with me?"

Ben stood and moved around the desk to face her. "He assumed you were married and living in Asterland. He used the money from the arrangement to pay for his treatment."

Jamie felt both relief and sadness. She had very much misjudged her father's motives. And she very much wanted to see him, to hug him, to tell him how proud she was of him that he was getting help. To scold him for not trying to contact her. "Will you take me to him?"

Ben rubbed a hand over his jaw. He wanted to do this for her, but he had promised her father to wait until he was ready. "He is not quite finished with his treatment, but he will be soon. I have made arrangements to return him here when he is released."

Her green eyes flashed anger, deep and penetrating. "I guess you've thought of everything, haven't you?"

How could he convince her that he had her best interest at heart? What could he say so that she would understand he still wanted her with every thread of his being?

Taking two steps forward, he touched her cheek. "I would very much like to report to him that he is invited to our wedding."

"No."

He took her into his arms, hoping he could weaken her resolve. "I am sorry. I do not mean to pressure you. All that I ask is for you to consider my proposal. I am willing to give you as much time as you need. I will see to it that the farm is put back in order for your father's return."

She wrested out of his arms and moved away. "He'll want to pay you back. And I insist you let him."

Ben's frustration increased. "I will not deny him that. But it will not be necessary if he is in my family. I protect my own."

A steady stream of tears flowed down her face. "Don't you get it? I don't want your protection. I don't need your money or your gifts. What I need is—" She shook her head. "Never mind."

"What do you need, Jamie, that I cannot give you?"

She swiped at her eyes. "I suppose you'll have to figure that one out yourself."

She slipped her hand in her jeans pocket and withdrew the ring he had so carefully chosen for her. Taking his hand, she placed it in his palm and closed his fingers around it. "Here. Maybe you'll find someone else who can wear this. Someone who's interested in your money and your station and your protection. That person's not me."

"I do not want it back."

"Neither do I." She turned away and headed for the door, but before she left, she faced him again. "The angels are beautiful, but I'll be returning those, too."

"I will not accept them. They are a gift to replace those you have lost." And he knew in that moment he had lost her.

"Fine. Thanks. As soon as my father returns, he'll be in touch about paying you back."

"And you will not see me again?"

"I can't, Ben. It's too hard."

He clung to the last of his pride, yet he must ask once more, but only once. "And you will not consider being my wife?"

Another rush of tears streamed down her face. "No."

He strode forward but kept his distance although the need to hold her, kiss away her tears, lived strong within him. But he would not let her leave until he had said all that he needed to say. "Should you decide that you need me, for any reason, I will be here for you."

"I appreciate it."

"You have my word, I will not bother you. If you change your mind, then you will have to come to me, for I will not ask anything of you again."

Then she disappeared out the door, out of his life.

He returned to his desk and sank into his chair. Tossing the ring aside, he rested his elbows on the solid surface and placed his head in his hands.

His chest constricted with the weight of his sadness, his remorse. He recalled his mother telling him that a shattered heart was the greatest pain anyone could endure, even a man. At the time, that concept seemed ludicrous. But that was before Jamie Morris.

Why could he not tell Jamie with words how he felt? He had been trained to be the best soldier. He had been groomed to be a proper prince. He had strived to be a learned businessman. Yet he had never been taught the ways of the heart, nor could he voice these strange emotions piercing his soul.

He had also learned when to accept those battles he could not win—and he could not win Jamie Morris.

That did nothing to ease the deep ache in his heart. No matter how long he searched, he would never find another woman who had touched him so.

But was he really so ready to give up this fight? His tenacity had seen him through difficult times. Would he simply walk away from something so precious?

He would have to consider that tomorrow. Tonight he had arrangements to make to return Jamie's father to her. At least then he would have some peace knowing that she would no longer be alone. Unlike him.

You have my word, I will not bother you. If you change your mind, then you will have to come to me, for I will not ask anything of you again.

Jamie had spent countless hours thinking about Ben's declaration, about him. Only moments ago she'd considered going to the ranch, telling him she'd been wrong. She wasn't sure what she would say. All she knew was that she needed to see him again as much as she needed air.

But he wouldn't want to see her unless she agreed to marry him. Could she do that not knowing how he really felt about her? She wanted desperately to believe he loved her. At times she truly thought he did. So why couldn't he tell her?

She shook her head. When it came right down to it, she hadn't told him, either. Maybe if she had, it might have made a difference.

The doorbell rang, and Jamie knew it was him. Prayed it was him. Now she would get her chance to tell him exactly how she felt. How much she loved him.

Slowly she opened the door, and discovered she'd been wrong. It wasn't Ben at all.

Sheer joy replaced the disappointment when she recognized the man standing on her porch. A man who had meant so much to her for so long.

His neatly combed silver hair, his careworn face were as familiar to her as the town she'd grown up in. He stood tall, his body still straight and strong despite the fact he had lived the life of a hardworking farmer and had suffered the loss of the woman he loved more than life itself.

"Daddy!" Jamie threw herself into her father's arms, hugging him tightly, crying some more even though she had mistakenly believed she was fresh out of tears.

"I missed you, baby girl." He set her back but kept his weathered hands braced on her shoulders. "My, my, you are a sight for these old eyes."

"So are you." She swiped her face with the back of her hand and tried to look stern despite the fact she wanted to shout with joy. "You've got a lot of explaining to do, Caleb Morris."

He dropped his hands from her shoulders, lowered his eyes and pushed up the sleeves of his faded chambray shirt. "Yeah, I know it. And I got a lot of apologizin' to do, too. So if you'll hear me out, I'd like to explain."

Jamie closed the door behind him and showed him to the couch, taking her place beside him.

"Are you feeling okay, Daddy?" she asked with concern once they'd settled in side by side.

He smiled. "Yeah. Better than I've felt in a mighty long while. Haven't had a drink in months."

"I'm so glad. But you're looking a little thin."

"I could say the same for you. You're as skinny as your mama when I married her." Sadness flashed across his expression and centered on Jamie's heart.

She hugged him again. "I know how much you still miss her, Daddy. I miss her, too. But she'd be so proud to know you've gotten help."

He clasped his hands in front of him and dangled them between parted knees, surveying the floor. "You know, Jamie girl, I ain't never held much stock in dreams, but your mama came to me in one right before I left. She told me to get on with my life in that voice she always used when I was late for supper."

Jamie smiled at the memory. "I can just imagine that."

"She mentioned you, too. Told me to take care of you. That's why I did it."

"You should have done it for yourself."

He slowly met her gaze, shame in his weary blue eyes. "Not the treatment center. I meant the wedding arrangement. I wanted you to have a better life than what I could give you. I figured if you got out of this town and moved to that Asterland place, then you could finally have the fine things you deserve.''

Jamie spoke through another rush of tears. "Oh, Daddy, I was happy just being your daughter. I'd have found the money to go back to school eventually, at least after you got back on your feet again."

"I wasn't sure that was gonna happen at the time. I know now that selling you into marriage to a man you didn't love wasn't a good thing. But I also thought that maybe if you didn't love him, you wouldn't hurt so bad if you lost him."

Jamie let the tears roll down her cheeks, unheeded. "I know now how bad that hurts, and I'm surviving."

He studied her with questions in his eyes. "Are you talking about that young man, Ben?"

She had no idea how much Ben had told him about the relationship, but she assumed he must have mentioned something. "Yes, I guess I am."

Caleb straightened and took her hands into his. "Are you in love with him, Jamie girl?"

This time she looked away. "'Fraid so."

"Well, I'd like to say I'm sorry about that, but I'm not." He tipped her chin up and forced her to look at him. "No matter how bad it hurt to lose your mother, I wouldn't take back one minute I had in her presence. She was a gift from God, that woman. I have peace knowing she sleeps with the angels."

"I understand that, Daddy, but I'm afraid Ben might not have those kind of feelings for me."

He frowned, deepening the lines around his eyes. "Are you tellin' me that man doesn't love you?"

She shrugged. "He's asked me to marry him, but he hasn't said he loves me."

Caleb let go a sharp laugh. "I didn't tell your mama I loved her, either. Not for a long time. In fact, I believe I finally said so one day down at the creek right after…'' He cleared his throat and a blush tinged his ruddy cheeks. "Never mind that. I just didn't know any pretty way to say it. Guess I was a coward.''

"Ben's no coward.'' Jamie was shocked at how defensive she sounded. She steadied her tone. "I'm just not sure how he feels about me because he's never really said.''

Rubbing his chin, Caleb stared off into space for a moment before returning his gaze to Jamie. "Well, now, I just spent the good part of two hours on one of them private jets with the man having a long conversation.''

Jamie's mouth gaped. "Ben?''

"Yeah, and all he could do was talk about you, what a fine daughter I'd raised. I barely got a word in edgewise.''

"Are you sure we're talking about Ben Rassad? Sheikh Ben Rassad?''

"He said his name was Ben. He had one of those curtains on his head and some kind of robe. Never seen a man wearing a robe 'cept at bedtime.''

"That would be him.''

"Well, since we're talkin' about the same man, I pretty much think that he does love you. If not, he's got one hellacious case of the flu 'cause he looked mighty lovesick to me. Sounded that way, too.''

Was her father right? Hope welled in Jamie's heart. "So he drove you over here?''

"Yep. After we got to Royal, he delivered me here himself.''

Jamie squeezed her father's hands. "And he just dropped you off?''

"Nope. He's downstairs waiting with one of his men. Said he wouldn't come up unless you said it was okay.''

Jamie's heart leaped into her throat. "I do want to see him. To thank him. But I don't want you to leave—''

Caleb stood. "Jamie, I'm plumb tuckered out from the trip. I need to get over to the farm and see what's what. Jeb and May Prentice have been seeing to the place for me, but I want to check it out myself."

"You could stay here. I mean, is that a good idea, going back to the place—"

"—where I lived with your mama all those years?" He nodded. "I'm to the point now where I can deal with those memories. She's still there watching over me."

Jamie rose from the sofa and drew him into another heartfelt hug. "You've come a long way. I'm so proud of you."

"I'm proud of you, too, Jamie girl. You're the one good thing I ever did in my life. 'Cept for marrying your mama. Now I'm going to head on back and give you your time with your fellow."

"Speaking of him, there's something you should know about finances and the farm before you go," she said hesitantly, afraid of his reaction to Ben's gesture. Her father had an abundance of pride.

"You mean the fact your Ben paid it off?" Caleb grinned. "He told me about it. Said I could pay him back when I took in the first crop. I still have some of that Asterland fellow's money left, too. Unless you think I ought to give it back seeing as how you didn't marry him?"

Jamie laughed through residual tears. "No, Daddy. It's yours to keep. Believe me, I earned it."

His brows drew down in confusion. "How's that?"

Jamie walked him to the door, anxious to see Ben now that her father was well on his way to recovery. "It's a long, long story. Too long to tell you tonight. But tomorrow I'll come by and fix you breakfast, then we can have a good long visit."

"Okay, then. That sounds mighty good. That rehab place

fed me slop I wouldn't even offer the hogs.'' Caleb leaned and kissed her cheek. ''I'll send your young man on up. I'm thinkin' you both have lots to talk about.''

''Yes, Daddy, that we do.''

Jamie watched her father head away, his gait quick and determined, so unlike the man he had become after her mother's death. She had so much to be thankful for. They both did. And she owed so much to Ben. She planned to tell him tonight. If he decided to come up.

Ten

Jamie leaned against the door for support and waited for Ben's arrival. She was dying to see him, to hold him, to tell him that what he had done for her, for her father, was more than anyone had ever done for either of them. To show him how much he meant to her.

A few minutes later, a steady knock caused Jamie to push away from the door, her pulse pounding in her ears.

She opened it to find Ben standing on the threshold wearing his traditional clothes and a killer smile, holding a bag from Claire's.

She nodded toward the bag. "What have you got there?"

"Dinner for two. Your father said he would not be joining us. J.D. has driven him home. I decided that Claire's would be preferable to my attempts at preparing dinner, although I would be willing to try again if you are willing to take that chance."

"With you cooking dinner?"

He pinned her with his gray eyes. "That, and other things."

"What other things?"

He sighed. "I would like to start over, Jamie. Prove to you that I am not the ogre you claim I am. Since you left me, I cannot eat or sleep. I cannot concentrate on my work. I can only think of what we have shared, how you felt in my arms. I miss your laughter. I miss the way your eyes light up when I touch you. I even miss your singing. So if you will grant me another opportunity to—"

Jamie grabbed his arm and pulled him inside, silencing him with a kiss. The bag dropped to the floor. She didn't care about food at the moment. She didn't care about the fact she was dog-tired. She didn't care about anything but Ben, the way he was kissing her back with such power that she thought her legs might not hold her any longer.

He hadn't said he loved her, but he was coming mighty close. And tonight, no matter what, she wanted to be with him, make love with him, even if it was only one more time.

As if he'd read her mind, he hooked his arms underneath her knees and lifted her up, much as he'd done that first night they'd made love.

Again she was swept away, not only by his powerful arms, but also by her feelings for him. Her love for him.

Once in the bedroom, Ben slid Jamie down the length of him and murmured, "I did not expect this reaction from you. I believe that you have missed me, too."

"Okay, I admit it. I have missed you." She couldn't seem to draw enough air into her lungs. "But I didn't expect this reaction from me either. I say let's just go with the flow."

He rimmed the shell of her ear with his tongue. "You

will receive no argument from me, but I have been traveling all day. I am in need of a shower.''

Jamie smiled up at him. "Me too.''

"Then perhaps that is where we should begin.''

"You don't have to tell me twice.''

Jamie slipped off her blouse and shimmied out of her slacks. Ben tossed his robes aside, raked the kaffiyeh from his head, then tore at the white shirt he wore underneath his robes, sending buttons pinging around the room like pea-sized gravel. After he snaked out of his slacks, they stood before each other totally naked.

The raw hunger Jamie saw in Ben's eyes made her shiver, made her want him right then, but she let him lead her into the small bathroom. He turned on the shower before bringing her against him for a long lingering kiss. A kiss full of promise and passion like none she had ever known before him.

Breaking the kiss, he took her hand and together they stepped beneath the lukewarm spray. They stood for another long moment and took in the sight of each other until Jamie began shampooing his thick dark hair, and he returned the favor. Covered in slippery suds, they laughed, they kissed, engaging in water play—a pleasant prelude to what would come next.

Jamie reached behind her for the shower gel, placed a few drops in her palm, then began to lather Ben's chest through the swirl of dark hair.

His sexy smile drove her to near insanity. "You would have me smelling like Alima's fresh-cut flowers?''

She returned his smile, sending her hands down his belly and farther still. He was completely aroused, and she was completely in awe.

"Are you complaining?'' she asked, tracing a fingertip down the solid length of him.

He sucked in a deep breath. "No. You will hear no complaint from me if you continue this."

She watched his features grow taut as she continued to caress him, memorize every inch of him. His eyes drifted shut and she knew he was close to coming unwound. Very close. And she felt such power.

Suddenly his eyes snapped opened and he circled her wrist in a steel grip. "Enough. You are driving me insane."

"That's the idea, Ben," she said, sounding incredibly coy.

"Not yet. As I said, this is only the beginning."

With that, he picked up the gel and spread some in his palms, then knelt down and washed her feet, one at a time. Jamie stared down on his dark head bent in concentration and realized that he was playing the role of slave. She had never expected that he would do something so subservient as bathing her feet. But then she had never expected to meet anyone like him.

He raised his gray eyes to her as he slid his large palms up her calves to the inside of her thighs, pausing just before he arrived at the point of her greatest need.

Standing once again, he took hold of her shoulders and backed her up against the cold tiles. He lowered his mouth to her breast and suckled one, then the other. Jamie moaned her pleasure, knowing it *was* only the beginning of his special brand of sensual torment. And she loved it.

He ran his hands down the curve of her waist, the flare of her hip, and cupped her intimately. "I belong here, Jamie," he whispered. "Inside you. One with you."

His masterful fingers delved into her needy flesh, making her quiver, making her beg. "Ben, please—"

"Shhh, Jamie. You need not speak. I know what you need. I can feel it."

Oh, boy, she could feel it, too. The steady building of

pressure, of heat, when he found her center and settled there. He continued to stroke her straight into oblivion. She cried out when he brought her to a climax so great she thought she might never recover. But she did, enough to scold him. "No fair. Now I'm ahead of you."

"Not for long, my Jamie." He brushed a kiss over her cheek. "Not for long."

Without bothering to dry off or turn down the lights, they made their way to the bed and sank onto the patchwork quilt, tangled together like clinging vines. They faced each other and continued to touch and explore, fondle and caress, until Ben said, "I can wait no longer."

Neither could Jamie. She craved the feel of his body inside hers. But when she tried to guide him to her, he moved away and left the bed.

Confused, Jamie sat up and found him rummaging through his pants pocket. "Ben, what are you doing?"

"I have brought the condoms." He slipped onto the edge of the bed and held up the plastic packets, at least five, for her inspection.

She couldn't repress a smile. "It doesn't matter."

He frowned. "I believe it does. At least to you. I want you to know that I will do whatever you wish of me."

She snatched the packets from him and tossed them aside. "I *wish* for you to make love to me. Now."

"Are you certain?"

"I've never been so sure of anything in my life."

Without words, he moved over her and sank into her waiting body, joining them on a level that went far beyond the physical. He moved slowly, with care, setting a perfect rhythm. Setting Jamie on fire with his increasing thrusts, his fine caress above the place where they were joined.

Suddenly he stilled and bracketed her face in his palms. "You are everything to me," he whispered. "You invade my waking hours. You have captured my heart.'' He kissed her softly. ''And I love you with all that I have to give, my Jamie.''

Had she heard him right? She couldn't find the heart to ask, afraid she had dreamed it.

''I have never known such feelings before,'' he continued, ''And I can no longer deny them.''

Tears of joys spilled from the corners of her eyes. ''You have no idea how much this means to me. For the longest time, I believed I was nothing more to you than a possession.''

His smile was so beautiful, so sincere, it brought fresh tears to her eyes. ''How could you be my possession when it is you who owns me?''

He kissed her deeply then. A kiss that held a promise for the future. Jamie knew right then that she belonged with him. They belonged to each other.

Again he moved inside her, touching her in places begging for his attention. Touching her heart and her soul. And when she could no longer hold back the tide of pleasure, she gave in to the release with abandon as Ben shuddered and called out her name.

In the aftermath, Ben turned to one side, taking Jamie with him. She brushed a wayward lock of damp hair from his forehead. ''My answer is yes.''

His smile was teasing and a little bit wicked. ''What would the question be?''

Obviously he wasn't going to make this easy for her. She couldn't blame him, considering how many times he had asked, and how many times she had refused. ''You know. The one you've been asking for a few weeks.''

''The one involving marriage?''

''Yes, that's the one. And if the offer still stands, then

yes, I will marry you and drive you crazy and have your babies.''

He cupped her face in his large hands. ''More than all the gold in the world, I want you to be my wife. I will put no one before you. All I need is the promise of your love.''

She held him tightly. ''Ben, I do love you. I think I loved you the moment you woke up in my bed that first morning.''

He kissed her gently. ''Then you will promise to wake with me every morning, and come to my bed every night? That you will be with me always?''

Never had Jamie felt such freedom. Such honest love. ''Yes. Always.''

He rolled her beneath him once again. ''Good. That is all I will ever need.''

Her tummy rumbled. ''How about food?''

He laughed then, a deep rich sound that made Jamie want to laugh, too, from the pure joy of it. ''Are you saying you are hungry?''

''Starving.''

His eyes darkened with intense desire. ''So am I, and after I am done with you, we can have dinner and plan our wedding.''

She was late, but not for the wedding.

Jamie still had forty-five minutes to get ready for the ceremony and about one minute before she would know if she was, in fact, carrying Ben's child.

Perched on the edge of the vanity stool dressed in her old terry robe, she stared at the white plastic stick resting near the sink and waited for the sign that would tell her yes or no.

A watched pot never boils.

Jamie released a nervous laugh when she recalled her

mother's words. She'd have to remember to teach Alima this particular American saying.

The remaining seconds ticked off while Jamie impatiently tapped her foot. Then suddenly, a plus sign appeared, leaving no doubt in her mind she was pregnant.

Pregnant.

She'd somehow known for a while that she was carrying Ben's baby. A baby created by two people who had found each other against all odds. Created by two people in love. Jamie felt truly blessed.

But when should she tell Ben?

She consulted her watch. Time was wasting. She still had to dress. Her father would be at the apartment any moment now to escort her to Royal's city park, the place they'd chosen for the ceremony.

After the wedding, she would tell Ben. This news could wait for now, until the right time. Until tonight, when they were alone. She didn't want anything to detract from this glorious day when she would marry the man she loved more than life. Just as her parents had loved each other.

Quickly she applied her makeup and curled her hair. Once she was satisfied with her appearance, she retrieved her mother's dress and slipped it on. A perfect fit.

Lovingly she caressed the white lace overlay. Funny, she'd told Helena last month she had no intention of wearing it anytime soon. Now she was wearing it and she was going to have a baby. Ben's baby. Things had certainly changed in her life in record time. And she couldn't be happier.

The doorbell sounded and she answered the summons, finding her father waiting for her. He looked so very handsome in his Sunday suit, his bright smile flashing against his tanned rugged face.

He held out his hands for her to take and smiled a proud-papa smile. "You look as pretty as your mama did when she wore that dress all those years ago. She would be so proud of you." A single tear drifted down his cheek.

Jamie tried to thwart her own tears with a smile. "Stop that right now. If I cry, I'll ruin my makeup, then we'll never make it on time."

He hooked his arm and she slipped her own arm through it. "Then let's not keep your Ben waiting," he said.

"No, let's not." She had kept him waiting long enough.

Ben stood beneath the gazebo waiting for his bride. The April day was unseasonably warm, and the tuxedo he wore decidedly uncomfortable. He supposed his discomfort had as much to do with nervousness as the weather. He would not be at ease until he had Jamie by his side. Not that he thought she would not show for the wedding. He was simply ready to begin their life together.

Matt stood nearby, speaking with fellow Cattleman's Club members Justin Webb, Aaron Black, Greg Hunt and Hank Langley. Moments before, Forrest Cunningham had walked away from Dakota Lewis who now remained back from the others, looking disinterested and perhaps a bit sad. Ben assumed he was contemplating the mission he would soon undertake in Asterland with his estranged wife. If luck prevailed, it would serve to bring the couple back together once again—as was meant to be, according to Aaron who had known them quite some time. Although the man denied any feelings for his wife, Ben and all the other members knew better. And Ben could certainly relate to Dakota's pain over not having his love with him. The short time he had spent without Jamie had seemed like centuries.

The statue of Tex Langley, the Texas Cattleman's Club's founding father, stood off in the distance. A crowd of on-lookers had gathered around the ropes that segregated sev-

eral rows of white chairs lined up on the lawn for the invited
guests. Ben assumed that a wedding between an Arabian
sheikh and a local woman would garner much interest in the
small town. At the moment, he wasn't concerned over the
masses. At the moment, he wanted to see Jamie.

The sound of a woman crying drew his attention. Alima
sat on the front row dabbing at her face, sobbing now and
again, much louder than most would deem appropriate. She
had told him that morning how honored she was to stand
in for his mother who was tending her latest grandson, the
sixth born to his brother. Alima's sobs grew louder when
the string quartet he had hired began to play. He believed
her tears were those of joy. Or perhaps the classical music
was not to her liking. At least she had come without the
blessed headphones.

Several guests turned to the direction of the street. A
spattering of excited voices acknowledged the arrival of the
white limousine pulling up to the curb.

Ben's heart vaulted in his chest and pounded in antici-
pation when he saw Jamie's father exit the car. And then
his bride slipped out in a flowing white dress. His Jamie.
His love. Soon to be his wife.

The guests who had been mingling began to make their
way to their seats, many noted citizens of Royal, including
several members—old and new—of the Texas Cattleman's
Club.

The Justice of the Peace moved to the gazebo next to
Ben, along with Matt Walker who would serve as the best
man. Matt's fiancée, Lady Helena, who would also bear
witness to their union, took her place on the opposite side.
The couple exchanged a look, one of love beyond all limits.
A few weeks ago, Ben might have scoffed at such a thing,
but now he truly knew the power of love. A love he had
never thought possible.

Ben turned toward the crowd and watched with pride as
Jamie made her way toward the gazebo. She walked with
grace and shone in the mid-morning sun like the fine jewel
that had brought them together. The mild breeze, smelling
of freshly mowed grass, ruffled her golden hair, ringed on
top by a circle of white flowers. The locks curled over her
breasts and glistened in the sunshine, bringing to mind that
day when Ben had first viewed her leaving the cleaners
with the dress she now wore, singing at the top of her voice.
That day that had nearly ended in disaster but instead had
brought them to this treasured point in time.

The dress flowed to the ground and fit her curves to
perfection. Ben mentally scolded himself when the image
of removing it slowly from her body filtered into his brain.

The quartet began to play the traditional "Wedding
March" as Jamie started up the aisle. Her smile was lu-
minous, giving Ben such a resounding joy. He had finally
made her happy, and it had taken not objects nor gifts, but
only a few simple words.

Once Jamie and her father had scaled the first of the two
steps, Caleb Morris turned and kissed Jamie on the cheek,
then offered her hand to Ben. "She's all yours," he said.
"Treat her like the gift she is, cause if you don't, I've got
a loaded .22 and a case full of shells." A grin melted his
serious expression.

A spattering of laughter came from the audience, and
Ben smiled in kind. Jamie looked mortified.

Ben bowed slightly. "You have my word, Mr. Morris."

Taking Jamie's fragile hand into his, Ben helped her up
the remaining step. When she met his gaze, he noticed a
fine sheen of tears in her eyes.

"Are you ready for this, Prince Ben?" she asked.

"I have been ready for weeks."

Jamie turned and handed her bouquet to Helena who smiled and said, "Amazing what love can do, isn't it?"

"Truly amazing." Jamie turned back to her soon-to-be husband and drew in a deep cleansing breath.

Debonair was the first word that had come to mind when she'd seen Ben waiting for her at the end of the aisle, dressed in a tailored tux, wearing his traditional kaffiyeh, looking strong and commanding. *Beautiful* was the second, and it much more aptly described him at the moment as she glimpsed the adoration in his gray eyes.

He brought her hand to his lips. "You are more exquisite than I could ever imagine."

"And you look much too good to be true."

The Justice of the Peace cleared his throat, signaling he was ready to begin the ceremony that would unite them forever. Not once did Ben look away, his voice clear and composed as he repeated the vows. Jamie wished she could say the same for herself. Her voice trembled, shaky with stubborn tears of joy that wouldn't go away. But she managed to get through it all the same.

Once they had exchanged rings, plain gold bands that Jamie had insisted on, the Justice of the Peace announced that Ben could kiss his bride. Ben cradled her face in his hands, and she slipped her arms about his waist.

"I love you, my Jamie."

"And I love you, Ben."

Then he melded his lips to hers in a long, lingering kiss that made Jamie forget where they were.

Fire rose to her face when everyone began to applaud and several hoots and hollers rose above the din.

Finally they parted and with hands clasped, walked back down the aisle to more applause. Once they were in the waiting limousine, Caleb and Alima joined them for the trip to the legendary Texas Cattleman's Club for the reception. When they settled in, Jamie and Ben on one seat, the housekeeper and the farmer on the other, Alima eyed Caleb from the top of his bolo tie to the tip of his shiny boots. But Jamie noticed Alima didn't look at all displeased by what she saw. Then Caleb shocked Jamie by smiling at Alima and introducing himself.

During the short drive, Jamie was content to cuddle with Ben in silence and listen to her father and Alima discuss Hank Williams and George Jones. Common ground shared by two very different people. Jamie could certainly relate to that.

They arrived at the club to much fanfare and hordes of people Jamie didn't recognize. She did, however, recognize the mayor, who greeted them inside the foyer of the Cattleman's Club. Jamie noted the plaque hanging above the entrance. Peace, Justice, Leadership. How well she understood that concept now that she had met Ben. He represented all those convictions, and much, much more.

Once inside the cavernous ballroom, Jamie could only stare at the flower-and-ribbon-bedecked walls, the fine crystal and china, the mammoth white cake graced by cascading pink roses centered in the middle of a long table surrounded by every kind of food imaginable. She'd never stepped foot in here before, and now she felt privileged to be among such honorable men. Privileged to be married to one of them.

Ben led Jamie to the table where Matt delivered a champagne toast and they performed the required cutting of the cake. Afterward, Ben introduced her to Aaron Black. She had already met his wife, Pamela, on the plane bound for Asterland, only now Pamela Black looked very different with her swollen belly and radiant smile, not a trace of the shy woman who had rarely spoken. Dr. Webb soon joined them with his wife, Winona, and a baby girl dressed in pink frills. Matt and Helena stood by, arm in arm, seemingly lost in their own world. Probably talking about their impending wedding, Jamie surmised.

Off in the corner, holding up the wall, was another man Jamie didn't recognize. He looked incredibly lost, and very, very distressed.

She tugged Ben's arm to garner his attention and discreetly pointed in the stranger's direction. "Who's that?"

Ben bent and whispered, "Dakota Lewis. Another member of the club."

"What's wrong with him? He looks like he's lost his best friend."

"That he has, I am afraid. I will explain later."

Her heart went out to the man. Right now she wanted everyone to be as happy she was.

After more conversation, Jamie's feet began to ache. She needed to talk to Ben alone, let him know she was ready to leave. Her stomach felt a bit queasy, and she wondered if a woman could have morning sickness in the afternoon.

When Matt and Helena walked away, Jamie grabbed the opportunity and led Ben into an alcove near a long hallway.

He took her in his arms and grinned. "Do you wish my attention, wife?"

"How perceptive of you, husband. Can we go soon?"

He nuzzled her neck, his warm breath playing against her already heated skin. "Are you growing impatient to begin our honeymoon?"

"You hit the nail on the head." He was also stirring up trouble when he sent a string of kisses down the valley of her breasts, exposed by the dress's sweetheart neckline.

"I am more than ready to make love to you," he murmured, along with a few choice words that would make the flowers wilt, just like Jamie's legs. "I believe there is a vacant conference room down the hall that should do quite nicely for what I intend."

She grabbed his ears and tugged his head up, away from dangerous ground. "I believe you are a wicked man."

He pressed against her, signaling loud and clear he was having some very wicked thoughts. "I am definitely a man in need of his wife's attention."

"Then let's get out of here," she said in a breathless tone.

"I will say my goodbyes, then we can go. I have made a reservation at the Royalton Hotel. I am sorry we cannot have a proper honeymoon until all is settled with Asterland."

Jamie didn't dare ask what was left to settle. She'd let him keep his mysteries. Besides, as far as she was concerned, Asterland could fall off the face of the earth. "I'm really sorry your mother couldn't be here."

He had the nerve to cup her breast through the lace. "I fear she is very taken with my new nephew." He bent and rimmed her ear with his tongue. "And tonight perhaps we can make her another grandchild."

Jamie couldn't have wished for a more perfect opening. But if he didn't stop fondling her, she wouldn't be able to speak. "Too late for that, I'm afraid."

Ben's head snapped up and he met her gaze. His hand slowly dropped to his side. "What are you saying?"

"I'm saying I took a test this morning. One of those over-the-counter things, not the lab kind. But they're supposed to be pretty accurate."

"And?"

Jamie smiled. "It said that Sheikh Hasim bin Abbas kadir Jamal Rassad of Amythra is going to be a daddy."

His eyes drifted from her face to her belly where he reverently laid his palm. "I could not have hoped for a better way to end this perfect day." He met her gaze, pure joy in the dark depths of his eyes. "Except, perhaps, by making love to you all night."

"As long as your son cooperates."

He looked at her with love shining in his eyes. "I am hoping for a girl. One with hair of gold like her mother, and a strong heart to match."

Jamie felt as though that strong heart might burst with all the love she held for this prince of a man. "It doesn't matter to me. I will love it, whatever it turns out to be."

"As will I, as much as I love you."

She circled her arms around his waist and stared up at him. "So when are we planning to return to Amythra?"

"This summer if all goes as planned. My mother will not tolerate waiting much longer to meet her American daughter-in-law, and my brother will want to hold another ceremony in honor of our marriage, if you agree."

"Whatever makes you happy, Ben." She worried her bottom lip for a moment, thinking she had so much to learn about his culture. "We've never really discussed it before, but where do you plan for us to live?"

"Here, in Royal. You should be near your father. We can visit Amythra as often as possible. And as soon as our child arrives, we can determine when you will finish your schooling."

Jamie wanted to cry again. "You'd do that for me?"

"I would do anything for you. I thought you would realize this by now."

She realized that, and how very much she loved him. Never again would she believe a person couldn't change. "But won't you miss your family? Your home?"

He took her hands into his and placed them to his lips. "For many years I have not known where home is. Now that I have met you, I know." He bent and kissed her softly, then raised solemn eyes to her. "You are my family now, Jamie. *You* have brought me home."

*   *   *   *   *

Watch for the final installment of the

**TEXAS CATTLEMAN'S CLUB:
LONE STAR JEWELS**

*when Native American retired Lt. Dakota Lewis
reunites with Kathy Lewis, his beautiful
estranged wife, and the ultra-secret
mission is completed in*

TYCOON WARRIOR

*by Sheri Whitefeather
Coming to you from Silhouette Desire
in May 2001*

And now for a sneak preview of
TYCOON WARRIOR,
please turn the page.

One

Retired air force lieutenant Dakota Lewis sat upright in a leather recliner, studying his home. Would the ranch look the same to Kathy?

Of course it would, he told himself a second later. He hadn't changed a thing. Not one cowboy novelty, not one Indian artifact. She would recognize every cow skull, every antler, every ceremonial pipe.

An ensemble of cedar, pine and mahogany made up Dakota's living room. He hadn't chosen pieces that belonged in sets. He preferred eclectic furnishings—hacienda-style trunks, tables topped with clay-colored tiles, mirrors framed in tooled leather.

He turned his attention back to his guests. They weren't discussing the mission at this point. Someone had made a reference to his wife. Was it Aaron Black? Sheikh Rassad? Dr. Webb? It wasn't Matthew Walker because Matt wasn't married.

No, but he was engaged. Happily engaged.

Hell, Dakota thought. What was wrong with him? The other men in the room were his friends, his peers. He had no right to envy them. They were all members of the Texas Cattleman's Club, the most exclusive gentlemen's club in the state. They were all wealthy—filthy rich, some might say. And they were all either happily married or happily engaged.

Yeah, all except for himself.

Dakota's estranged wife was due to arrive at his ranch any minute. Kathy had left three years before, a choice she hadn't even bothered to explain. Dakota had come home from an assignment to find her gone. Two years of marriage shot to hell, and Dakota didn't know why. He had loved his wife, was certain she had loved him, too. Yet she'd walked out on him, saddling him with an emotional wound festering deep in his gut.

A wound that had become exceptionally active today. The top-secret mission the Cattleman's Club's members had come to discuss involved Kathy. She was the foreign service consul being teamed with Dakota. Together they would fly to Asterland, a small European country on the brink of a revolution.

The doorbell rang. Dakota excused himself from the other men and strode toward the entryway. Checking his watch, he tightened his jaw. Thirteen hundred hours. She was right on time.

Kathy stood on the other side of the door, slim and elegant, her thick, hard-to-hold hair coiled in a neat chignon. She wore a beige pantsuit and an emerald blouse that intensified the color of her eyes. Cat's eyes, he'd always called them. Cat's eyes and fire-tinted hair, features that belied Kathy's proper nature.

Neither spoke. Instead their gazes locked, and they stared

at each other for what seemed like the longest moment of Dakota's life.

"It's good to see you," she said finally, extending her hand.

Polite pleasantries, he thought. What else could he do? This was business, and Dakota viewed his work as the number-one priority in his life. He wouldn't let anything stand in the way of an assignment, not even the pain shooting from his gut to his heart.

"It's good to see you, too," he responded, clasping her hand as though her touch wouldn't affect him. It did, of course. Her hand felt small and feminine, her skin soft and warm against his own.

He invited her in, cursing the memories threatening to surface. Her fragrance drifted to his nostrils like fresh strawberries smothered in cream. Kathy preferred scented lotions to heavy perfumes, aromas that never failed to make Dakota hungry.

Suddenly he fought the temptation to uncoil her hair, let it fall across her shoulders. He hadn't forgotten the woman he loved, hadn't forgotten how she looked soaking in the tub, the fiery tendrils slipping free from the pins that secured them, her long, sleek body creamy and smooth.

How many times had he carried her, soaking wet, to their bed?

"Dakota? Are the others here?"

Kathy's question jarred him back to reality. Damn it. He stood in the tiled entryway, his hormones battling for control. How in the hell had he let that happen?

"Yes, they're here." He escorted his estranged wife to the living room, hating himself for the moment of weakness.

Like the Texas gentlemen they were, the other men rose as Kathy entered the room. Aaron Black came forward to hug her. How easily Kathy embraced Aaron, Dakota thought, wondering why a fist of rivalry gripped him hard and quick. Not only was Aaron blissfully married with a baby on the way, he was also a good friend, the American diplomat who had introduced Dakota to Kathy nearly six years before.

Kathy shook hands with the others, and soon they settled into their seats.

As Kathy crossed her legs, Dakota poured her a ginger ale from the wet bar. He didn't stop to ask her preference. He knew what Kathy's favorite soft drink was, and he still stocked the bar with it.

She thanked him quietly, the ice in her glass crackling. He poured himself a cola, opting to keep his hands busy. The urge to loosen her hair had returned.

How different they were, he thought, how opposite. Kathy was renowned for her grace and diplomacy, whereas Dakota was as rough-hewn as his taste in furniture, often solving matters with force.

Lifting his cola from the bar, Dakota took a swig, wondering if he should have spiked it with rum—something, anything to take the edge off. How could a woman skilled in conversation walk out on her husband without the slightest explanation? How could she ignore what they had meant to each other? The love? The passion?

Dakota didn't need to ask Kathy where she had been for the past three years. He already knew. She had gone to Washington, D.C., to serve in the Bureau of Consular Affairs, leasing a spacious apartment in an exclusive suburb and furnishing it with antiques. Prior to that, she had been on an extended leave of absence, debating whether to end her career. For Kathy, living abroad in the foreign service had become stressful. She wanted to remain in Texas. Or so she'd said.

Regardless, locating her in Washington had been easy. Keeping his distance had been the tough part. But Dakota figured Kathy didn't want to be confronted, didn't want him standing on her doorstep, demanding to know why she had left. So, consequently, Dakota's pride—his hard-baked masculine ego—had managed to keep him at bay.

Sheikh Rassad drew Kathy into the meeting, pulling Dakota in as well.

"Are you familiar with the events leading up to this mission?" the other man asked her. "Are there any details that are not clear?"

"Aaron briefed me," she responded. "I know the lone star jewels were stolen. And I'm also aware that they've been recovered." She sat with her usual graceful posture giving the sheikh her undivided attention. "Albert Payune, The Grand Minister of Asterland, masterminded the robbery, and he intended to use the jewels to fund a revolution. Which is where Dakota and I come in. It's our job to make sure that revolution doesn't happen."

The sheikh leaned forward. "Aaron informed us that you are well acquainted with the king and queen."

"That's true. I'm very fond of the royal family, and I don't intend to see them lose their country." She placed her glass on a coaster, sending the sheikh a reassuring smile. "I've already made arrangements for Dakota to accompany me to Asterland for the queen's birthday ball. And since he will be visiting as my guest, his presence won't arouse suspicion."

Dakota listened, although he had already been briefed by Aaron. The plan had been carefully orchestrated. Dakota's initial arrival in Asterland must appear to be of a personal nature. And what could be more personal than traveling with his wife? They wouldn't need to fake their cover, at least not on paper. They would be playing themselves.

Almost.

They would have to pretend to be in the midst of a reconciliation, a couple mending their marriage.

Dakota glanced at Kathy, and she barely returned his gaze. She appeared poised and professional, but he could sense her uneasiness. The same uneasiness that swept through him.

How were they going to pull this off if they couldn't look at each other? Couldn't relax in each other's presence? Dakota glanced at Kathy again, his chest constricting with a familiar ache. Somehow, someway, they would have to. The future of a country was at stake. And this mission was far too risky for errors.

Silhouette® *Desire*®

invites you to enter the
exclusive, masculine world of the...

TEXAS
Cattleman's Club
Lone Star Jewels

**Silhouette Desire's powerful miniseries features five
wealthy Texas bachelors—all members of the state's
most prestigious club—who set out to recover the
town's jewels...and discover their true loves!**

MILLIONAIRE M.D.—January 2001
by Jennifer Greene (SD #1340)

WORLD'S MOST ELIGIBLE TEXAN—February 2001
by Sara Orwig (SD #1346)

LONE STAR KNIGHT—March 2001
by Cindy Gerard (SD #1353)

HER ARDENT SHEIKH—April 2001
by Kristi Gold (SD #1358)

TYCOON WARRIOR—May 2001
by Sheri WhiteFeather (SD #1364)

Available at your favorite retail outlet.

Silhouette®

Where love comes alive™

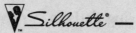

SILHOUETTE® MAKES YOU A STAR!

Look in the back pages of all June Silhouette series books to find an exciting new contest with fabulous prizes! Available exclusively through Silhouette.

Don't miss it!

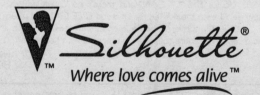

Silhouette®

Where love comes alive™

P.S. Watch for details on how you can meet your favorite Silhouette author.

Visit Silhouette at www.eHarlequin.com   STEASER

January 2001
TALL, DARK & WESTERN
#1339 by Anne Marie Winston

February 2001
THE WAY TO A RANCHER'S HEART
#1345 by Peggy Moreland

March 2001
MILLIONAIRE HUSBAND
#1352 by Leanne Banks
Million-Dollar Men

April 2001
GABRIEL'S GIFT
#1357 by Cait London
Freedom Valley

May 2001
THE TEMPTATION OF
RORY MONAHAN
#1363 by Elizabeth Bevarly

June 2001
A LADY FOR LINCOLN CADE
#1369 by BJ James
Men of Belle Terre

MAN OF THE MONTH

For twenty years Silhouette has been giving
you the ultimate in romantic reads. Come join
the celebration as some of your favorite authors
help celebrate our anniversary with the most
sensual, emotional love stories ever!

Available at your favorite retail outlet.

Where love comes alive™

Visit Silhouette at www.eHarlequin.com   SDMOM01